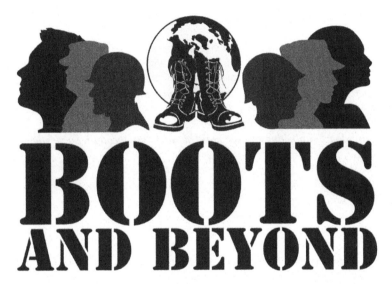

BOOTS AND BEYOND

Stories of Trials, Tragedy, Triumph, and Transition

LaJocha Polati

**Boots and Beyond:
Stories of Trials, Tragedy, Triumph, and Transition**

Copyright © 2021 by Michele Irby Johnson

All rights reserved. No part of this book may be used or reproduced by any means, graphic, electronic or mechanical, including photocopying, recording, taping or by any information storage retrieval system without the written permission of the publisher except in the case of brief quotations embodied in critical articles and reviews.

One Kingdom Publishing books may be ordered through booksellers or by contacting:

*Michele Irby Johnson
www.iam-mij.com
www.onekingdompublishing.com
(301) 453-4770*

Because of the dynamic nature of the internet, any web address or links contained in this book may have changed since publication and may no longer be valid. The views expressed in this work are solely those of the author and do not necessarily reflect the views of the publisher, and the publisher hereby disclaims any responsibility for them.

Any people depicted in stock imagery provided by SPJ Graphics are models, and such images are being used for illustrative purposes only.

Cover Design by SPJ Graphic Designs || spjgraphicdesigns.com || (301) 720-2039

ISBN: 979-8-9850350-0-1

Printed in the United States of America

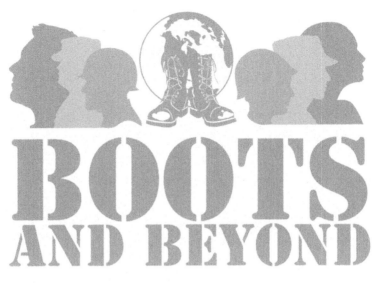

Copyright © 2021 by Michele Irby Johnson. All rights reserved.

Table of Contents

CO-AUTHOR DEDICATIONS i
I SALUTE YOU vii
INTRODUCTION ix
A VISIBLE REMINDER OF THE HOLY 1
ACCEPT AND FOLLOW YOUR ALLOTTED PATH 15
FROM THE WARDROOM TO THE CLASSROOM 27
HE OUTRANKS THEM ALL 39
I AM A RESILIENT WARRIOR 49
IT WAS ALL GOOD…UNTIL 61
LIVING IN THE DARK WITH PTS 69
MENTAL MADNESS 79
PLAN AND PURPOSE 89
RESILIENCE UNDER FIRE 101
TEARS BEHIND A FITTED MASK 113
THE DAY I RETIRED, LIFE BEGAN 125
YOU ARE STRONGER THAN YOU COULD EVER IMAGINE 135
About the Visionary 145
Other Literary Works by the Visionary 151

CO-AUTHOR DEDICATIONS

Leasia L. Brooks

I dedicate this book first and foremost to God, Who always provided the ram in the bush. Without Him I would not have made it. To my comrades, who believed in me, stood boldly and unashamedly by me in the roughest of times. And last, but not least, to my dear husband for your unconditional love and support in allowing me to go after my dreams beyond the boots. I truly love and appreciate you all!

Tangella R. Brown

This "segment" is dedicated to my mother, Olevia Brown and my father, Samuel Brown who have always supported me in ever endeavor, great or small. They have been my greatest advocates and cheerleaders and thought that I could do anything I put my mind to. I left home at an early age and never really returned for 30 years, but they always wanted their baby back home so here I am and I'm dedicating this book to you with all my love.

Ossawa F. Gillespie

I dedicate this book to my wife, whom over the years – through the trials and tribulations – has remained that piece I always wanted in my life and even more of things I did not know I needed in my life. Your love and support have given me strength for things I thought I was incapable of achieving. Thank you for believing in me and pushing me to strive for my dreams.

Dr. Stacy L. Henderson
This book is dedicated to my husband and children for whom my love is immeasurable. Throughout my journey in the U. S. Navy, your love was my lifeline when I found myself treading in rough waters. Your unwavering support continues to make my navigation through life worthwhile. What a blessing to have a family 'anchored in love.' I am eternally grateful to my parents, family, friends and loved ones who were sound examples and strong shoulders when I needed them most. Each of you is a blessing to me. My love for you is overflowing. To God Be The Glory!

Curtis "Gunny" Jones
This book is dedicated to my family and friends. To my mother who will tell you what she did every day in the Corps with me and didn't sleep until I retired! To my wonderful wife who has stood by my side for over 39 years and helped me weather this dark storm that has been named PTSD! For she has seen me at what I would call my lowest points and helped me to return! To my children who told me that I should write a book one day. Last, but not least, to my "Brother Bloods!"

Sonya Mills-McCall
I dedicate this book to my late mother, Georgia Mills Foster and my father, William "Coach" Mills, who instilled in me the importance of education, good work ethics, and family. To my son, Colin, for it was your death on March 24, 2021, that taught me to not put off for tomorrow what I can do today. You will forever be my "Teddy

Bear!" To my living children, Tara, Tavien, and Tene' – you all are my heartbeats. It is because of you all that I live and breathe. Each of you have given me something different, yet the same. In your own ways, you all taught me different ways of growth, responsibility, and commitment. I am grateful and humble to be your mom.

Raphael J. Holmes

I would like to say a special thank you to my mother, sisters, entire family, and friends. All of you made serving in the Air Force much easier through all your love, support, and prayers. I truly appreciate all of you and couldn't imagine my life without you. I love you all with my entire heart. I dedicate this chapter to all of you. I would also like to dedicate this chapter to every service member, past or present. Your fight and sacrifice will never go unnoticed, and I will forever be thankful for your service to our country. An abundance of great blessings to you all.

Erin Owens Weatherly

I dedicate this book to my husband, Cedric, and my children, Janelle and Cedric Jr. You have given me life and a reason to continue my journey. My life is brighter with you. To my parents for providing me a foundation and my strong will. To my village that has given me support through my trials & tribulations. Saving the best for last, to my God...thanks for loving me unconditionally and guiding me to complete Your will.

LaTorcha R. Polati

I dedicate this book to my loving husband, Fabio Polati; to my beautiful daughter, Kianna Grant; and my rock (my mother) Jennie J. Winn, who together have been the pillars of support that have kept me from giving up when all looked like it was lost. Each of you played such an important part in holding and supporting me as I reconstructed myself into the woman I am today. Fabio, your love carried me; Kianna, your love strengthened me; and Mommy, your loved guided me to fight through this thing called life that wanted to keep me down and out. Thank You!

Kevin K. Richardson

I dedicate this writing first, to God for having a "Plan and Purpose" to everything. To my Wife, Celeste, who has faced every challenge and remained solid. To my grown children, who make me laugh. I would not be who I am if it were not for God and each of you. Lastly, to those who I spent time with over both, my military and ministry travels over these combined 40 years.

Bobby J. Spear

I dedicate this book to my mother and father, whom by an example provided me life examples on how to always respect and treat people. I also wish to dedicate this book to my wife, Don Sheree Spear and my children Blair and Donald, who endured my absence due to requirements of military deployments and extensive travel for the U.S. Secret Service for Protective Details and Investigative requirements. I'd like to recognize those fellow 'comrades in arms' who have mentored me and those I have had the pleasure leading and mentoring.

Stephen A. Tillett

I dedicate this book to the largely unseen men and women of our military who serve the families of recently killed U.S. military members at the Air Force Port Mortuary. They serve with selfless excellence and dedication. They receive and escort the flag-draped "transfer cases" containing our fallen service members. They greet, console and pray with grieving family members, and they perform the necessary restorative work on our fallen troops in preparation for final military honors. In spite of the "weight" of the work they do, they maintain a vibrant esprit de corps that lightens the load on every man and woman serving at the Mortuary. My fondest wish for every military family and every Soldier, Sailor, Marine and Airman is that one day "They shall beat their swords into plowshares, And their spears into pruning hooks; Nation shall not lift up sword against nation, Neither shall they learn war anymore."

Katriana R. Walker

I dedicate this book to the Lord, and I pray it brings Him Glory, Honor and Praise. I, also dedicate it to my father, Norman Walker for teaching me unconditional love and how to stand in the face of adversity. Finally, I dedicate it to every person who took the time to listen, cultivate, pour, and share their wisdom with me along my journey. And above all, to every person I ever hurt in my brokenness... I'm so sorry and I sincerely ask you to please forgive me.

Boots and Beyond: Stories of Trials, Tragedy, Triumph, and Transition

I Salute You

To all my fellow servicemembers who paved the way for men and women of all races, ages, nationalities, religions, and walks of life, I stand in your footprints and *salute you!*

To all my new fellow servicemembers who have recently enlisted and have sworn an oath to protect and defend our country against all enemies both foreign and domestic, welcome to the ranks! You are needed!

To all my fellow servicemembers who have given of themselves fully to ensure the safety, honor, and glory of our country, and continue to serve, *I salute you!*

To all my fellow servicemembers who have come through the ranks, honored their time and commitment, and have since separated or retired from duty, *I salute you!*

To all my fellow servicemembers who paid the ultimate sacrifice with their lives in service and defense to our Nation, *I salute you!* You are not forgotten!

To all my fellow servicemembers and co-authors who have agreed to share their stories with the world through this literary work, I am forever grateful for your contribution, and *I salute you!*

INTRODUCTION

MSgt (Ret.) Michele Irby Johnson, Visionary
Speaker | Trainer | Consultant | Coach | Entrepreneur
Published Author | Talk Show Host | Pastor

When an individual commits to serve his or her country, that commitment is followed by the sacrifice of self – life and limb – family, career, dreams, and anything else associated with the "raising of your hand." An undeniable bond is forged between the military member, their colleagues in uniform, the mission, and the Nation as a whole. Donning the uniform and the boots evokes a sense of pride in knowing that your commitment is to protect your country, your neighborhood, your family, and yourself. Saying 'yes' to the uniform often means saying 'no' to yourself, but the benefits that accompany such a selfish posture cannot be compared when you put it all into perspective of having such an amazing opportunity to stand armed to fight the enemy at any cost.

This is not to say that the career of a military member is always brimming with bouquets of roses and stringed instruments playing, but the reality is that this call to serve is often laced with disappointment, trials, challenges, regret, fear, tragedy, as well as triumph. With the turn of each year or the elevation to each rank brings with it the need to contemplate the 'yes' that one echoed during their swearing in ceremony before heading off to basic training. For some, the journey has been enjoyable and packed with all they had imagined, while for others the journey has been a long rocky road of unexpected twists and turns.

As a young girl, I loved visiting my grandmother a couple of weekends a month and besides remembering the living room furniture engulfed in plastic, I remember seeing an 8x10 framed photograph of my father in an Air Force uniform. I would sit and admire that photo and I would say to myself, 'one day I'm going to go into the military just like my dad.' Little did I know that at the age of 21, I would find myself sitting in an Air Force Recruitment Office asking all the intelligent questions about joining the military. I was sold and with that image of my father in my mind, I enlisted in the United States Air Force in 1987. I was a novice to the realities that my military career would eventually bring.

My military career was colorful to say the least. Each year, each reenlistment revealed something new, something different in varying degrees. For the most part, I absolutely loved my life in the ranks. From basic training and beyond, I was pegged as a leader because I could see where the "cracks" were that needed to be repaired in order for the troops to survive and to thrive no matter what they faced along the way. I was driven and focused, and I had a determination to succeed, and I wanted everyone around me to do the same. Little did I know that I would have to follow my own recipe for triumph in my own career. My story highlights the heartbreaking events that led to my untimely retirement.

Take my personal story, for instance...

"READY OR NOT...RETIRED!"

Michele Irby Johnson, MSgt (Ret.)
United States Air Force
*Operation Noble Eagle, Operation Enduring Freedom,
Operation Iraqi Freedom, Operation New Dawn*
(1987 – 2012)

"Though he slay me, yet will I trust in him: but I will maintain mine own ways before him." (Job 13:15)

My military career afforded me the opportunity to serve in a number of capacities. My first assignment was as a Non-Destructive Inspection Specialist/Journeyman for 13 years, where I was responsible for inspecting all aircraft to ensure the safety of the equipment as well as the pilots. I worked in conjunction with several other maintenance shops to safeguard our assets (jets) and our pilots. My second assignment was as a Training Manager for about four years, where I was responsible for tracking the training deficiencies and needs of approximately 430 troops within our unit. My final assignment was with the Chaplain's Team for nine years, where I served as the NCOIC (Non-Commissioned Officer In Charge). My journey started at the rank of AIC (E-3 Airman First Class) and ended at the rank of MSgt (E-7 Master Sergeant). I was proud of my trek as an airman. It was not a smooth road, but it was one of appreciation, joy, and immense honor and pride…But that would soon take a turn that I would not soon forget!

Upon my return from a lengthy deployment in the Middle East, I was faced with the reality that my regular Wing Chaplain was on a lengthy assignment out of state. Positioned in his absence was a female chaplain, who would cover the ministry team until he returned. At first look, things seemed to be on the up and up and that this "fill-in" would be one that the team could embrace and follow in the short-term. As reality set in, it became apparent that this female had underlying issues and motives that would be revealed over time. I began to notice how driven she was and how hard she was trying to impress Command. Now, I understand that going over and above is not a crime, however, when it is done to the extent that no one and nothing else matters, it becomes a problem.

I started to see the competitive expressions of this Chaplain who would often forget what her purpose was in uniform…*Integrity First, Service Before Self, and Excellence In All We You Do!* It somehow seemed that she only wore the cross on her uniform, but she did not carry its tenets in her heart and spirit (at least not from the perspective of those she covered on our team or in the unit). With each interaction with this female, there seemed to be tension. It was as if she did not like anyone who knew who they were or had confidence in their knowledge, skills, or abilities. She had no appreciation for the fact that I was just as driven, determined, intelligent, and forthright as she was. Now, I was in no manner disrespectful, but as the one who had been in the office and managing the office for eight years prior to her arrival, I knew what was going on from all directions. She would often dismiss my familiarity with the unit and would advise me to do something that I KNEW had already been done and failed or she would micromanage my every move as if I had no clue as to how to do my job. Believe me, I was not the only one who picked up on these antics. Others in the office noticed how she operated and soon began to avoid any formal interactions with her. Some decided to leave the unit, seek other opportunities, or contemplated getting out altogether because she was quite the handful.

I often found myself doubling back to make sure that I did what I said I did and followed through on every directive. I was questioned when I wanted to make up time or serve my weekends or training days only to be met with pushback to "let me know in advance when you make such requests..." (although the requests were typically made a month in advance because by this time I was living out of state and had to plan my travel and billeting for my weekend stay)...But I digress. By this time, I was studying and preparing for the rank of SMSgt (E-8 Senior Master Sergeant), knowing that this rank would require that I had to changes jobs or change locations. I had spoken with my First Sergeant, who encouraged me to prepare for the exam and then we would seek where the new rank would place me.

The straw that broke the camel's back for me came when this female cancelled a scheduled deployment that I was assigned to take. When I was originally contacted about the deployment opportunity, I was excited and awaiting further instructions as I had for my previous deployment. Typically, there was a team that would reach out and provide step-by-step guidance to ensure that everything was in order prior to deployment. I know that I had to be cleared for my PT (physical training), but I had contacted the medical doctor to inform her of my latest surgery that hindered any type of bending at the waist, running, etc. and I was granted a deferral. When this female chaplain contacted me, she stated the obvious about my PT test and I explained to her the details, but that I would be good a month or more before the deployment.

The next thing I knew, I was receiving an email with the subject line: DEPLOYMENT CANCELLED! Quite naturally, I was caught off guard and I questioned how this could be, seeing that no one from the Deployment Office contacted me. As it turns out, this female chaplain had been privately communicating with someone outside of our unit and God only knows what she was saying "on my behalf" and I find out about the cancelled assignment via email. I promptly and professionally responded stating, "The same way that I was emailed to be informed that my deployment was "cancelled," the same measure of communication should have been used several months prior to investigating my status for the deployment and the necessary requirements and be given an opportunity to at least give explanation of my "overdue PT" status."

This incident became the hailstorm that snowballed out of control. From this point on, working under this female became unbearable. It had gotten to the point that she had scheduled a meeting without my knowledge with the Chief. In my follow-up contact with the Chief, I requested that he and I meet privately because I wanted to "speak freely" about how the morale in the Chaplain's office had dropped considerably since this female took over. I even suggested that some of the remaining troops under my supervision feel free to meet with the Chief to express their concerns regarding this female as well. He agreed to meet with me as well as the other enlisted to get a bead on the climate in the office. After this meeting, the foolery continued with the female chaplain to the extent that everything I did was heavily scrutinized. She would make changes to completed tasks and then add "to be changed at the Wing Chaplain's discretion," after it had been distributed to the team. Her reasoning was that she wanted to make sure that I was "pulling my weight," often forgetting that I was supervising five enlisted troops under me, ensuring our other Chaplains were cared for, and keeping the office afloat at the same time. What eyes was she using to view my contribution? Evidently, they were clouded with power and her desire to steal the Wing Chaplain position from our REAL Chaplain who was away on assignment.

The next thing I knew, I was informed via email that I was on "the Forced Management Retirement pool." What in the world did *that* mean? Had this female stooped to sadistic depths to get me out of the military? Yep! That is exactly what she did! I was in shock! I was confused! I was hurt! Had she been that threatened by me that she would do this? Yes, yes, and YES!!! There was no open discussion. There was no meeting. There was no heads-up. There was nothing, nada…crickets! My soul sank that day at the reality that my military career was in the hands of a witch in uniform… a poisonous snake in the ranks who sought to move up in power no matter who she stepped on, stepped over, spit on, or otherwise 'S-d' on! I could not believe it! Was she that power hungry? Was she that insecure? Was she that vindictive? Absolutely!

The next thing I knew, she was trying to be chummy with me, being unusually cordial. I did not know who this person was. She was like Dr. Jekyll and Mr. Hyde! She was a narcissist dressed in BDUs, touting blessings out of a two-sided mouth. As she spoke to me through an insincere smile, I just stared at her and had nothing to say. I simply could not believe it. She had me added to the retirement list... She was that twisted that she would leave the office without a qualified NCOIC. She left new troops to fend for themselves without a supervisor. She dismissed the only SME (Subject Matter Expert) from the team before a major unit inspection. The troops would call me after I was gone to get help and direction but were soon told not to contact me. She was stubborn and content enough with *her* decision to let the team implode.

My official retirement date was July 10, 2012. After 26 years of faithful and honorable service to my country, and my many failed attempts to plan a joyous exit, there was no retirement ceremony. There were no commendations. There was no cake, no flag, no songs sang... NOTHING! I and my 26-year career just faded into the background. Other than the people in the Personnel Office who had to process me out of the unit and the Retention Office, no one knew I had retired. Surprisingly, about one year after this forced retirement situation, I was contacted by a military comrade who shared with me that there was an opportunity to return to the IMA Ready Reserves Team. This, of course, would take some work to "unretire" me and put me back in boots. Unfortunately, by the time this communication arrived in my inbox, I had two service-connected disabilities and had gained an excessive amount of weight. While I would have jumped at the opportunity at any other time, I recognized that my reality did not align with my hopes of wearing the uniform again.

As my truth settled in my heart, I grieved the loss of something that I once honored…something that I cherished deeply. Depression had settled in, and I felt like I had been thrown away and that my contribution to my country meant absolutely nothing. No more deployments. No more trainings. No more temporary duty assignments. No more PT Tests. No more military camaraderie. No more celebrations. No more "war games" in preparation for unit readiness inspections. No more promotion through the ranks. No more uniforms…No more boots.

Today, whenever I see a service member in uniform – no matter the branch of service – I celebrate them even though I still grieve the loss of my military career. If I had my way, I would still be in the service until my true retirement age of 65. There remains in the back of my closet one pressed set of BDUs and one set of Service Blues as a reminder of something that I loved so dear. On the shelf sits my last pair of combat boots… There was a time that seeing these items would make me cry uncontrollably, become physically sick, and deeply depressed as I relived those horrible events that led me to my untimely retirement. Today, I can finally look at these items without breaking down in actual tears (though my heart still sinks). That is not to say that I do not still feel the sting of what happened, but I can look at these items with a sense of pride and accomplishment. I look at my life as it is today, and I am grateful that my military career prepared me for every facet of my life… the good, the bad, the indifferent… the fair and the unfair. My career taught me tenacity, courage, and resilience! My career showed me that my faith was stronger than those who fought against me. I have learned how to fight with character, integrity, and grace, understanding that *"the battle is not yours [mine], but God's"* (2 Chronicles 20:15b).

I have learned how to be an encouragement to myself and to others, through my tears and disappointment. I have learned that even though everyone may not be for you, that God is for you and there are others who truly want the best for you. I am encouraged by the words found in Romans 8:31, which declares *"If God be for us, who can be against us?"* I am forever grateful to God Who has helped me to embrace the honor of serving my country and others… I am forever grateful to God Who has strengthened my resolve and helped me to live a blessed and successful life…beyond the boots!

Tenacious Transition…

Michele Irby Johnson

A Visible Reminder of the Holy

Stephen A. Tillett

I consider myself fortunate and blessed to have served my country as a chaplain for twenty years. I began my career as a First Lieutenant in the DC Air National Guard on December 14, 1996. I retired as a Lieutenant Colonel on January 1, 2017. During those 20 years, I had the opportunity to deploy with my troops and go to trainings both in the continental United States (CONUS) and outside of the continental United States (OCONUS). I concluded my military service in a special duty assignment at Arlington National Cemetery as an Air Force reservist.

My intention, when I accepted the offer to contribute to this book, was to focus on the rotation that I served at the Air Force Mortuary Affairs Operations (AFMAO) at Dover Air Force Base in Delaware in 2010-2011. However, the events that propelled us into the *need* to have an enlarged presence in Delaware began nine years prior on September 11, 2001. As a result of that very critical day in our nation's history, I was able to serve in several different capacities. So, before I address my time in Delaware, let's look at the beginning.

On Tuesday, September 11, 2001, I was working in my home office in the attic of the parsonage in which we lived at Mount Zion United Methodist Church in Baltimore, Maryland. My wife called up the stairs to tell me to look at the TV because a plane had flown into one of the buildings at the World Trade Center. At that time, we thought it was probably a small plane flown by an inexperienced pilot. We would soon find out the story was entirely different as the details of the attacks on the World Trade Center in New York, the Pentagon, and the plane that crashed in Pennsylvania became more comprehensive. It appeared to be a coordinated attack on our homeland, so I was pretty sure my presence, in uniform, might be required. I received a call that afternoon asking me if I could be available to come serve in the Pentagon community. I said, "*If* I can be available? Our country is under attack. I will be right there."

For the next three and a half months, I served as a chaplain ministering to our military and civilian personnel in the Pentagon community. That service began working in the family resource center, which was stood up to care for the needs and concerns of family members who were anxiously awaiting news about their loved ones. Unfortunately, in most cases, the news was not good news, but we had to wait to confirm our worst fears.

There was one evening early in my assignment that I will never forget. The husband of one of the missing civilian employees at the Pentagon I had met earlier in the day contacted me and asked if we could have a conversation. It was late in the evening, but he was awake and so was I, so I stopped by his room, and we talked for more than an hour. Calvin (not his real name) was very distraught that his wife might not be recovered alive, and he just wanted to talk. Early in the recovery process it is a "search and rescue" mission. After a certain amount of time passes, however, it becomes a recovery effort when no further signs of life are detected. Every now and then a miracle occurs and someone alive is pulled from the rubble but, sadly, that would not be the outcome in this case.

Calvin and I discussed his wife who was obviously the apple of his eye and the love of his life. He referred to his wife as "Duchess," because she "was better than a queen and more valuable than a princess." He talked about their courtship, their family, and the plans they had for their future together. The two of them had been on the phone just before the attack and he was hoping against hope she might have survived and just needed to be found, alive, in the rubble. He even managed to gain access to the recovery site as our first responders were working feverishly to find anyone who was still alive.

The rescue workers teams were compassionate and decent enough to allow him to remain on-site as they searched. In fact, on the day President Bush came to the Pentagon, rather than having him leave the site, which was becoming a much more secure site and crime scene, over time, they had him to hide himself in one of the

Port-a-pots, until the president and media had left. After that he was able to continue to remain on site a little while longer. The human cost of these attacks on September 11th was apparent to me from the very beginning. It continues to manifest itself from time-to-time from then until now.

One of my cousins, Major Reginald Mebane was an officer in a nearby courthouse in New York City. As a Vietnam vet and Purple Heart recipient, running towards the danger was nothing new to him. In fact, an account of the actions of Reggie and his fellow officers were detailed in the book, *Running Toward Danger*, written by Cathy Trost and Alicia Shepard, which included a picture of Reggie covered in ash. He and ten other officers from the courthouse ran down the street to help evacuate civilians from the World Trade Center area. Three of his officers lost their lives that day. While Reggie survived that day, he ultimately lost a battle to a rare form of lung cancer caused by the debris he was covered in and ingested that day. The effects of 9/11 continue to manifest in one way or another on a daily basis.

Among the most agonizing stories I heard were those of the persons who were in the Pentagon that morning who survived the attack. As I conducted a Critical Incident Stress Debriefing (C.I.S.D. or C.I.S.M. (Management) with a group of survivors, the practice begins with everyone telling their story. One man said, "Honestly, I'm tired of telling this story over and over again." The thing that stuck with him the most was hearing the voices and screams of people on the other side of a wall, but he was unable to get to them. He was even able to get a couple of people out of the building, but then he went back to try to save more. He was haunted by the screams of those people he couldn't save. In fact, one of the more humanizing testimonies I heard a few times was how people use to walk around that massive 6.5 million square foot building and be so busy with their work that they would scarcely notice the other people as they passed in the halls. However, after 9/11, they had a newfound appreciation for seeing each other. When they said, "It's good to see you!" they meant it. It was as if they were saying, 'I'm really glad to see you… that you're still alive!' I wonder if now, twenty years later, that they still take that extra second or two to speak with one another and recognize one another's humanity, or if things have gone back to "normal."

One other exchange was especially meaningful for me among months of meaningful times of sharing and conducting. One day a young Navy/Marine officer came to me at the end of a group CISM briefing to schedule an appointment. When he came into the office, he was *clearly* shaken. As we talked, he revealed that he was having difficulty sleeping, which is normal after a traumatic event. Part of his issue sleeping revolved around a recurring dream where his young daughter was in danger, and he was not able to save her.

He was attempting to "be strong" and not burden his wife with what he was feeling. I suggested to him that she was probably also trying to "be strong" and not trouble him with whatever thoughts, fears and concerns were going on in *her* mind. I recommend that he and she have a conversation where they share what was *really* going on with them and that they cry together or whatever they needed to do. Then they could truly lean on each other to try to recover from the event. The next time I saw him a few days later, he was like a new man. He was more like himself again. He said that he went home and took my advice, and they did indeed share and cry together and found their strength and sustenance in one another. I am sure there are any number of other stories like this from the people who survived that day and have continued to live, love, and serve this country to the best of their ability.

After that high intensity introduction to the stressors and other elements of the longest war in US history, I now want to reflect some on the time I spent at "The Port" — Air Force Mortuary Affairs Operations (AFMAO), formerly known as the Port Mortuary. My time there literally occurred at the halfway point in that war in Afghanistan and marked "the end" of the war in Iraq, though a smaller number of casualties would continue to occasionally come from Iraq for several more years.

The human cost for the decision to invade Iraq, a country that did *not* attack us and had nothing to do with 9/11, was incalculable.

Estimated numbers of Iraqi war dead, close to half of whom were civilians, is several hundred thousand. The number of US military killed during that war was close to 5,000, and the number of the wounded numbered over 32,000. As I have told people about my time at Dover, "whenever you hear a report about some bad news and casualties over in Iraq or Afghanistan, they are coming to Dover AFB."

At AFMAO, Chaplains served in one of three areas connected to the Mortuary. We all spent some time in each of the three areas of responsibility. Processing is where the bodies were received after the Dignified Transfer was completed on the tarmac. It was here that the human cost of the war was the most palpable. I continue to be in awe at the resilience of the young people who served in that assignment. Imagine how difficult it must be to receive the remains of someone who is as young as you are. That was a challenge that many of the young troops had to face. They were encountering fallen Soldiers, Marines, Airmen and Sailors, some of whom were in their early 20s just like some of the young people serving so capably at the Mortuary.

The ministry of chaplains in that environment was in part to care for the morale and emotional and spiritual health of military members and civilians serving in that building. There were any number of conversations/informal counseling sessions that took place as we all wrestled with the enormity of the work we were called to do. We also sort of functioned as morale officers and arranged for excursions and other activities for military members on their days off, just to provide a change of pace during their time at AFMAO. One of the more notable excursions was a White House tour that everyone enjoyed.

The most obvious public and ceremonial tasks performed at Dover were when the planes landed with the remains of our military members, and occasionally civilian contractors. The flag draped transfer cases were provided with a Dignified Transfer to vehicles that awaited, so they could be delivered to Processing for the work that had to be done there. On many occasions, politicians would come to greet the families and honor the military members who were returning to US soil for preparation, final military honors and burial. On occasion, even the President or Vice President might come, or a high-ranking official from the Department of Defense.

Our ministry on the tarmac, irrespective of the weather or the hour, was to march out to the plane containing the transfer cases, render the appropriate military salute and offer prayer. In addition to praying for the souls of those killed in combat, we also prayed for their families and for all the other military members and civilians involved. There was a lot of waiting in this area of our duty, as the arrival times of the planes would sometimes "slip" depending upon weather and other delays. Thus, the old military adage, "hurry up and wait."

The most significant personal interaction we had with family members took place either in the Center for Families of the Fallen, or occasionally in the Fisher House for Families of the Fallen where family members would be housed when they came to Delaware to witness the Dignified Transfer of their loved ones. We spent a lot of time in the Center awaiting word that the planes had arrived and were ready for families to come out to the tarmac and witness the Dignified Transfers. It was amazing to witness the faith, patriotism, grace and even humor our families who had just found out their loved one had lost his or her life within the past two or three days. Family members and friends would come to share their stories and fond memories. Occasionally those memories would result in some laughter. I distinctly remember a conversation with a family from Alabama who were discussing the rivalry between the University of Alabama and Auburn University football teams. I asked the family members, "how do you decide who you're going to root for?" Their response, without missing a beat, was that decision was made "at birth!" It was a family inheritance that you were born into. I remember appreciating the laughter in the room that evening as a temporary lifting of the weight for the reason we were there.

Some of the senior leaders in the Air Force chaplaincy always told us that we, as Chaplains and Chaplain Assistants, were a "Visible Reminder of the Holy." Never was that more apparent than in the sacred assignment at the Port. I do remember one family that

I encountered while serving in Delaware. It was a Saturday afternoon, and I was driving on the base. I don't remember exactly where I was heading. It might've been to the bowling alley or contemplating where I was going to get dinner. But I saw several people in a car who were driving as if they did not know exactly where they were going. My guess was they could have been looking for housing on the base in order to receive their loved one. So, I asked them if they needed some help and they told me where they were trying to go. I led them over to the mortuary where they were informed of the time schedule. The mortuary was closed for the evening but would resume service the next morning. Their loved one was a retired military member who was serving as a contractor overseas. He had died of a heart attack, and they had come to receive witness of his return to American soil. They went into town to find a hotel space and then we all went out to dinner together. I was buoyed by the love and support that this family displayed toward one another and the great respect they had for their big brother, a retired Marine, who continued to serve his country as a military contractor. As the evening was winding, down his younger sister and his girlfriend asked me to "look out for their brother" while he was at the Mortuary. And so, the next morning I followed him from the time the transfer case was opened, through the autopsy and the other services that were provided for him to prepare him to go back home to Georgia. His sister and I remain in occasional contact to this day, via Facebook. That underscores the most meaningful portion of the work we were privileged to do. The privilege of providing comfort, a shoulder to cry on or a listening ear...The honor to be a Visible Reminder of the Holy, and to occasionally establish meaningful and memorable relationships with those we served. I only wish that more of our fellow Americans could learn to truly "see" and appreciate one another as the folks at the Pentagon did after 9/11. And I hope and pray that we can recover or discover those aspects of our lives that make us "United" and allow us to work together and support one another, even in the hardest of times, whether we agree about everything or not!

Rev. Dr. Martin Luther King, Jr. said that *"We must all learn to live together as brothers, or we will all perish together as fools."* I have seen the power of common purpose and a shared understanding of the strength and power of our collective when we decide to "live together." I pray that we never lose that. It is the tie that binds us together in this great *American Experiment*, one American to another. Lord willing, sooner than later, we will begin to see each other, again, as a "Visible Reminder" of what it truly means to be an "American."

CHAPLAIN STEPHEN A. TILLETT, Lt. Col. (Ret.)
United States Air Force
Operation Noble Eagle, Operation Iraqi Freedom,
Operation Enduring Freedom, Operation New Dawn
(1996 – 2017)

Stephen Andrew Tillett is a pastor (31 years), husband, father, son, author, talk show contributor, community leader and retired Air Force Chaplain. Lt Col Tillett served as the Wing Chaplain for the 113th Air Wing at Andrews Air Force Base, Maryland, where he functioned as the senior pastor for a "congregation" of over eleven hundred men and women. In January 2009, he was the Command Chaplain for the National Guard troops supporting the Inauguration of President Barack Obama. He served a "rotation" at the Air Force Mortuary Affairs Operations (AFMAO) at Dover AFB in Delaware. His final military assignment was as the Senior IMA Chaplain in a

Special Duty Assignment at Arlington National Cemetery until his retirement on 1 January 2017.

"Pastor T" has served as a pastor in his hometown, Washington, DC, Baltimore, Maryland and, since July 2004 in Annapolis, Maryland. He is a published author of *Stop Falling for the Okeydoke: How the Lie of "Race" Continues to Undermine Our Country* (2017), which has received numerous favorable reviews. He is also the author of many articles and columns in local and national news publications. During his tenure, he served as the president of the Anne Arundel County Branch of the NAACP. He is now a Clergy Co-Chair for ACT (Anne Arundel Connecting Together) an IAF affiliate. Stephen Tillett is also a daily contributor on "The Lavonia Perryman Show" (910 AM Superstation, Detroit, iHeart Radio) as a political analyst.

To experience his work and ministry, visit:
www.StopFallingForTheOkeydoke.com
www.AsburyBroadneckUMC.org

ACCEPT AND FOLLOW YOUR ALLOTTED PATH

Bobby J. Spear

My name is Bobby J. Spear, a retired Chief Master Sergeant in the U.S. Air Force/Air National Guard and my career spanned over 32 years of combined Active Duty and traditional Air National Guard, to include activation after September 11, 2001. I also served as a member of the U.S. Secret Service for 26 years prior to retirement. I was a recipient of continued blessing in two fabulous careers. I will convey how each position I was blessed to obtain was built upon for the next. Each position or rank led to more and more responsibility and capability.

Many of my life choices seem to me to be pre-ordained. As you read my chapter, I will do my best to convey to you how each job I had positioned me for the next... My journey to a top enlisted rank in the U.S. Air Force 'Chief Master Sergeant' and that of a Supervisory Operation Support Technician in the U.S. Secret Service. Fifty years ago, I began my journey and adventure as a member of the U. S. Air Force. Going into the Air Force was one of the best decisions I could have made, of which I've never had any regrets.

My military experiences began when I enrolled in college at Jacksonville State University in Jacksonville, Alabama and had to do Army Reserve Officer Training Corps (ROTC) as a freshman, a requirement for Freshmen at the time. As an ROTC member, I joined the Pershing Rifles (Drill Team and Fraternity); this was short lived as I did not stay the whole year. I only completed one semester before I was notified of my low draft number and that I had a high probability of being drafted into the Army. This alone with my not being ready for college studies pushed me further toward the U.S Air Force in the footsteps of my oldest brother.

Army ROTC was my first introduction into military discipline and dedication. My short time in ROTC for one semester prepared me for my future military career in the Air Force. My Air Force career began on March 11, 1971. This is when I left home alone for the first time as well as my first aircraft flight. When I started my basic training, the Training Instructor (TI) selected me as one of four squad leaders because of my prior experience in college ROTC.

As a Squad Leader, I became responsible for twelve other individuals. I enjoyed having the responsibility for the wellbeing and military bearing of other Airmen. Air Force basic training back then only lasted for six weeks. Upon graduation from basic, two monumental factors occurred: My first promotion from E-1 to E-2 and starting my primary Air Force Specialty Code (AFSC) Job Training, where I was still to train on Lackland AFB in Law Enforcement (LE). I must admit that that first promotion felt like I was a year older in only six weeks' time. This is when my TI said to me that I clearly had the tools to be a Chief if I remained in the Air Force.

I soon transferred to the other side of the base to continue training as Security Police/Law Enforcement Specialty. Upon arrival for LE training, there were not enough personnel to constitute a full class. So, I was then given the Flight Chief title and responsibility of receiving all newly assigned personnel. I assigned dorm rooms, helped to get mailboxes, and ensured that a class was ready and capable. Here I enjoyed having responsibility and being able to help others to be ready for their Air Force career. While in the Security Police Academy, the Air Force Honor Guard came around recruiting personnel; they deemed me sharp enough to join their ranks. With my prior background as a member of the Pershing Rifles in college, I made a good candidate and accepted their offer.

I traveled to Washington DC to be a member of the esteemed Air Force Presidential Honor Guard. Here, as a member of the USAF Honor Guard Drill team, I was promoted to my first Noncommissioned Officer rank as an E-4 Sergeant. Beyond just doing my job, I participated in such milestones in a young Airman's life. I stood watch around J. Edgar Hoover's coffin in the Rotunda of the Capitol as part of the Marine Watch (Midnight to Morning), was a Body Bearer for Former President Lyndon Johnson, traveled to Independence, Missouri as part of the Joint Military Cordon for the funeral of Former President Harry S. Truman, and then the

Inauguration of President Nixon for his second term. Each of these events introduced an uninformed kid from Alabama to world and national news events.

In the Honor Guard, I learned how to position myself for promotion opportunities. I carried throughout my career lessons learned when assigned to the USAF Honor Guard. Those lessons are patience (as in 'practice makes perfect'), the audience doesn't see your endurance during practice, the dropped weapons, being stabbed by your teammate during weapons movement, enduring extreme climates (in the 70's we trained outdoors in hot and hand freezing cold weather), polishing boots and low quarters to a high gloss, ironing fatigues twice a day, every day. But the most important lesson learned is staying true oneself and loyal to your teammates.

After three years in the USAF Honor Guard, I asked for a transfer to work as I was trained as a Law Enforcement Specialist to determine if I would reenlist in the active Air Force. I was told my new base would be Andrews Air Force Base in the DMV (DC, Maryland, Virginia) area, but my new assignment was to Hill AFB, Utah. This was my final base during my first enlistment (March 1971 thru March 1975). From March to June 1975 I was home in Alabama to determine my next steps. This is when I decided I didn't want to go back into the Air Force. I decided to go back to Washington, DC.

I applied for several Law Enforcement agencies during this time. I applied to most Federal agencies. The US Capitol Police were the first to respond. I was invited to come in for an interview in July. Upon my arrival for my interview with Capitol Police recruiting office, the interviewing officer advised me that I was disqualified due to my weight. At the time, I weighed 203 pounds; the standard for my height according to him was 189 pounds. Now, this was confusing and quite disappointing because as he was explaining my problem, I'm looking at his approximately 300 pounds to 330 pounds frame barely fitting into his chair. Like my early military career, once again what I applied for I didn't receive. But, in this disappointment was my allotted path through God's grace. Not more than two weeks later, I was contacted by the U.S Secret Service.

I went to the US Secret Service personnel for my first interview. Although the USSS personnel knew I was interested in the Uniform Division (UD) at the White House, she steered me toward the Treasury Department Police (TDP) after telling me that UD had no open positions (a few years later I learned that she had lied). I later worked with and became a supervisor of a friend who was offered a UD position months after I was told there was no openings. I won't offer an opinion on whether she was racially motivated, but he was not a veteran and White. The Treasury Department position was paying several thousand dollars less than that of the UD.

At the time I was being promoted to Sergeant at TDP, I decided to join the District of Columbia Air National Guard. I had run into a subordinate at TDP in military uniform while we were in training at Federal Law Enforcement Training Center (FLETC). She along with a close friend from my Honor Guard days made me long for that military camaraderie. At this point, I began my dual tracking security career. As I was promoted to E-5 Staff Sergeant in the Air Guard, I was one of four TSF Sergeants who were transferred within the Secret Service to a different position. I was now employed as a Special Officer providing physical security and dignitary protection. This was also the time the tasking for the Air Force Security Police career field was changing to just security.

I spent two years as a Special Officer and soon applied for the Operation Support Technician (OST) position at the USSS Washington Field Office in a quasi-investigative position. This was the only position I actively sought, and it was the one of two best positions I worked. As I progressed at the USSS, I was dual tracking with the DCANG. As the security career field was changing responsibilities from internal base security to Air Base Security, the emphasis was on external base security. During these transitions my responsibilities and promotion continued. The unique thing about the Air Guard is that often one's promotion is contingent upon the unit having an open position. So, you either waited for someone to leave, retire, or get promoted themselves to free up a slot before you can fill open position.

In the mid to late 1990's, both of by career duties and responsibilities mirrored each other. I was selected as the Supervisory Operation Support Technician with duties as the Operations Manager, supervising Operation Support Technicians and Communication Specialist/Dispatchers. I scheduled duty assignments recommended and coordinated training courses, established liaisons and, worked with other Law Enforcement agencies and civilian vendors providing services to the U.S. Secret Service - Washington Field Office. I also provided 'Integrated Logistics Support' for office Administrative, Investigative and Protective operations. Also, during this span, I became the Security Forces Manager (Chief Master Sergeant/E-9), where I directed personnel, managed resources and activities, interpreted, enacted and enforced policies, and applicable directives.

As I mentioned before, these positions and promotion during my careers, each allowed me to utilize lesson learned from each. I was able to utilize my military leadership skills to complement my leadership skills in the USSS. I took extreme pleasure in helping to get personnel promoted in the Guard and being able to monitor the strength, desires, and capabilities of my team members. Most of my positions were the result of my unchartered path that I believe I received with blessings of God. I built upon what was needed for me to be the best at my allotted position and availed myself ready for what would be next.

I was working preparations for the 2002 Winter Olympic much of 2001 when 9/11 happened. I was at Ronald Reagan National Airport working a protective detail for Former President George H. W. Bush. My day started early and got even longer with the two attacks. I was in my office when I saw the second aircraft hit the second tower. I knew then that this wasn't a misguided lone aircraft situation. I immediately made my way to the WFO Communication Center (Duty Desk), using my years of training in Airfield protection, to position various Special Agents for quick response due to the alert that there was a fourth aircraft headed for the White House. I also was able to connect WFOs Protective Operations with the 121st Command Post (F-16 Fighters) working in the Washington, DC air apace.

In 2002 after the Winter Olympics was over, I was activated where I was tasked, directed, and performed security and force protection duties to include: directing defense of personnel, facilities/plant protection, equipment, and resources from hostile forces to include a deployment in 2003 for Iraqi Freedom. At my home station, I provided crisis management, emergency preparedness, and continuity planning for emergencies. I acted as Senior Advisor to the Commander on all issues affecting the Squadron. Other jobs/position I acquired after retiring using my military and Secret Service experience were Lockheed Martin Program Manager – Integrated Logistics Services, Integrated System Improvement Services – Regional Director, and Potomac Recruiting – Managing Director Federal and Military. I'm currently volunteering as a Cub Scout Master, and Veterans Treatment Court Mentor.

BOBBY J. SPEAR, CSMgt (Ret.)
United States Air Force
*Vietnam Era, Operation Noble Eagle,
Operation Enduring Freedom, Operation Iraqi Freedom*
(1971 – 2005)

Bobby J. Spear is a US Air Force/Air National Guard retired Chief Master Sergeant who is also a U.S. Secret Service retiree. He is a husband, father, grandfather, VETERAN'S TREATMENT COURT MENTOR, recruiter, and résumé (New Horizons Career Services) writer. He is also a Former Managing Director Federal and Military with Potomac Recruiting, Former Regional Director at Integrated Systems Improvement Services, LLC, Former Program and Hiring Manager with Lockheed Martin, Former Program Manager at US Air Force Security Forces DC Air National Guard, Former Security Forces Manager at DC Air National Guard, and a

Former Technical Support Supervisor at US Secret Service. He ENCOURAGES Veterans to reach their full capability and purpose in transitioning to civilian employment. He assists transitioning veterans in TRANSFORMING their military experiences and skills into a civilian résumé listing their military skills and capabilities in a civilian format.

FROM THE WARDROOM TO THE CLASSROOM

Dr. Stacy L. Henderson

So, there I was relaxing on the sofa in my home office one Tuesday evening after dinner. I was reading a copy of *A Piece of Mine* by J. California Cooper, one of my favorite Authors, when my cell phone rang. I did not recognize the number, but I answered it anyway. It was an unexpected notice about a job; a chance to teach Navy Junior Reserve Officers Training Corps (NJROTC) at a Chicago-area High School. My friend Regina had been teaching NJROTC at Proviso West High School in Hillside, Illinois for three years after she retired, and she loved it. I wanted to teach there also, but no position was available, so I concluded that it wasn't meant to be. Besides, I was happily retired from the U. S. Navy after an amazing 20 plus year career. I was traveling quite often and visiting some of the places that I had Ports of Calls in during my various deployments at sea. There were several places on my 'Bucket List,' and I was determined to visit every single one. Aside from 'globetrotting' I was busy running Dr. Stacy L. Henderson & Associates Coaching and Consulting, LLC, my faith-based firm that I established in 2004, while still on active duty. I planned to start and run my *own* business after retirement, but by the Grace of God, I made the right connections, got a college education, and tapped into the resources needed to launch it while still serving on active duty.

I sat up and listened as Dr. Gregory Horak spoke to me about a job opening for that school year in August 2015, which was just a few weeks away. I thought to myself, *"Stacy...do you really want to go back to work full time? What about running your own business and being your own boss? What about...?"* By the time we ended our conversation, I had decided to go in for an interview, although I thought that there was no way they would hire me once they found out I was teaching Sunday School and Youth Bible Study, running a business, volunteering in the community, a Board Member of the National Women Veterans United, and I was on my second consecutive reign as the National Queen of the Montford Point Marine Association, Inc., *etcetera, etcetera, etcetera.*

The National Montford Point Marine Association, Inc. is a non-profit organization established to 'Preserve the Legacy' of the first African Americans to enlist in the U. S. Marine Corps. It is because of them that my father, the late Staff Sergeant Robert Henderson, Sr. became a Marine. And, of course, being a 'Daddy's Girl,' I followed in his footsteps and joined the military, carrying on a proud family tradition of generations of military service men and women.

After our conversation, I went back to reading my book, but I could not focus on the content. I love teaching and was interested, but I had never taught in a high school. I laughed out loud as an image of me as a teenager popped into my head. I had a LOT of big dreams and plans for my life. I became a mother at age seventeen when my daughter, KeiSha, was born a few weeks before my Senior Year in High School. After graduation, I went to Savannah State College (now University), our hometown HBCU, on a Youth Futures Academic Scholarship while waiting to enter the Navy. About a year later, I got married, and within two years my husband and I welcomed our son, William. Balancing family, a military career and college proved extremely challenging.

All these years later, I now found myself living alone in my mid-forties...an *empty nester*. As much as I love being a mother, both of my children are now 'grown and on their own.' They send me an allowance and call and visit often enough to make sure I'm doing well. Reflecting on motherhood I thought, maybe I could teach at a high school because teenagers have good energy, and they keep me on my toes. They are creative and innovative. This new generation of Millennials and Generation Z-ers are challenging, but intriguing.

I left the book on the sofa, took a deep breath, and slowly exhaled. Then, I stood up, and with my cell phone in my hand, I went downstairs to the kitchen. I opened the refrigerator and stood there with the door open for at least ten minutes, frozen in place, while trying to figure out what to eat or drink. Honestly, I don't think I was even hungry. I was lost in a daze wondering how to proceed. I closed my eyes and asked, *"Lord, what should I do? Please give me a sign."* At that moment, my friend Maxine called which interrupted my thoughts. She said, *"Girl, you were on my mind so I'm checking up on you. What city, state or country are you in today - or have you left earth altogether and finally made your journey to Mars?"* We both screamed with laughter. *"Maxine, don't start with me. Believe it or not, I'm at home considering teaching NJROTC,"* I said. She gasped and yelled, *"That is perfect for you! You're such a positive influence on our youth and they would learn so much from you. Besides, you teach Sunday School and Youth Bible Study. Your students love you and enjoy being in your class. That age group is challenging, but you make it look easy. And besides, you raised two teenagers and they turned out just fine. You can restructure things at the firm, travel less often and fit a full-time teaching job into your schedule."*

The more she spoke, the better I felt about it. She was right; I do love young people and we could actually learn from each other. I asked her, *"Really, Maxine? Do you really think I can do it?"* Her response was classic, *"Yes ma'am! In fact, I know you can do it. They need you and you need them."* I told her, *"Thank you. I have a few things I need to do before my interview, which is in two days. I'll let you know how it goes. I love you, Girl."* She replied, *"I love you, too, Ma'am!"* Maxine is always encouraging and supporting me. Even when she disagreed with me, she told me the truth – what I needed to know NOT what I wanted to hear. Ever since the day we met on the USS WASP (LHD-1) while deployed during Operation Iraqi Freedom, we have been close friends.

I realized that I was still standing in front of the open refrigerator. I took out a bottle of Brisk Lemon Tea, took two slices of bread from the breadbox on the kitchen counter, got the peanut butter, grape jelly, and a saucer from the cabinet, along with a spoon from the drawer. I made myself a sandwich and sat down at the kitchen table, ate it slowly and sipped my tea. Ever since I was a child, a peanut butter and grape jelly sandwich has been my favorite snack. It was my comfort food, especially when I found myself in a tough situation.

After my snack, I went back upstairs, drew myself a warm bubble bath, lit a few candles and grabbed *A Piece of Mine*. I went into my master bathroom, disrobed and took a long, relaxing bath while reading my book. I laughed and I cried. The stories were so powerful and engaging; they took me on a range of emotions. By the time I finished my bath, my skin was wrinkled. *I was in there for nearly two hours!* I got out and got ready for bed. I said my prayers, turned on the television with the volume low and slowly drifted off to sleep. I had barely started to dream when I clearly heard my late mother's voice say... *"Stacy, you left the refrigerator door open."* I sat up in bed and said, *"Thank you for reminding me, mama. I love you and I miss you."* As tired as I was, I crawled out of bed, stepped into my fuzzy slippers, and took a slow walk downstairs. I stood in front of the open door at least five minutes before closing it. Then, I turned on the light above the stove and slowly walked back upstairs to my bedroom. I stepped out of my fuzzy slippers, crawled back into bed, pulled the covers over my head and cried myself to sleep.

When I woke up the next morning, the sun was shining brightly through my bedroom window. I looked at the clock on my nightstand: 0837 (8:37 am). I stretched with satisfaction after such a good night's sleep. Then, I got out of bed, went through my daily hygiene routine, threw on some workout clothes and went downstairs and ate a bowl of oatmeal with raisins and a little bit of 2% milk. Afterwards, I went for a 3-mile walk before running errands. Then, I treated myself to a few hours at the *Nouveau Riche Spa* for a fresh French Manicure, Seaweed and Strawberry Pedicure, a full-body deep tissue massage, a haircut, a facial and I had my eyebrows arched. After leaving the spa, I treated myself to dinner at Red Lobster: Cheddar Bay Biscuits, clam chowder, an Ultimate Feast, a slice of Key Lime Pie for dessert and a Mango Pineapple Smoothie. Okay, I had two slices of key lime pie...but...I walked three miles earlier so the extra calories didn't count, right?!

After dinner, I headed home for an evening of relaxation because my interview was tomorrow. Once inside, I went upstairs, took a warm shower, got dressed for bed and turned the television on with the volume low. I went to bed early because I needed to wake up 'before the sun rises and the rooster crows,' as we say in the South. One of the many things I loved about growing up in Savannah, Georgia is the fact that Gullah Geechee people have a saying for *everything*. Most of the phrases are like riddles but are easy to remember. However, some of them can be difficult to figure out. Whenever I heard one that I couldn't decode, I would ask my mother (Mary) and she'd say, *"Stacy, just keep on living. You'll understand it better, by and by."* In other words, there was more to come...

I turned in around 2000 (8:00 pm) that night with excitement in my heart and a smile on my face. I was looking forward to tomorrow. I still lived in Military Housing at Naval Station Great Lakes, about a two-hour drive from the school where the interview was being held at 1000 (10:00 am). So, I needed at least eight hours of sleep. I was not sure what to expect, but one thing was certain: God was up to something. I prayed silently before drifting off to sleep.

I woke up around 0600 (6:00 am) on Thursday after a deep sleep. I started my daily routine and after a light breakfast of wheat toast, a hardboiled egg, three strips of bacon and a glass of cranberry juice, I prepared myself for the interview. I drove the distance listening to Gospel Music by CeCe Winans playing softly. Still unsure about the prospect of teaching NJROTC, I said aloud, *"Oh, mama, I wish you were here because I need your help figuring this out. Daddy would say, 'Go for it!' but I know you would have a saying perfect for a time like this."* I laughed at myself, talking to and about my parents aloud, but it comforts me. I kept driving down the 94 East Tollway until it ended at the juncture of the 294 South Tollway. As I coasted along toward the South Suburbs of Chicago, I heard my mother's voice clearly say, *"Stacy, when it's the right time, and you're in the right place, you'll receive the right blessing."* There she was...even now...she was still speaking to me in riddles.

I arrived at the school thirty minutes early. My late father was a U. S. Marine and he always said, *"If you're early, you're on time. If you're on time, you're late."* So, in true military fashion, I was there early; dressed to impress in my Summer White Uniform, with my ribbons, Warfare Pins, Rank and name tag placed perfectly. I parked in front of the building and walked up the sidewalk leading to the front door. Standing at the bottom of the steps leading into the school, I heard a still small voice whisper, *"For, I know the thoughts that I think toward you, saith the Lord, thoughts of peace and not of evil, to give you an expected end."* The words of Jeremiah 29:11 spoke to me with clarity. I ascended the stairs and pressed the buzzer to be granted access.

Once inside, I walked slowly but confidently to the top of the stairs which surprisingly lead to the NJROTC Classrooms. There, I met Lieutenant Commander Edward Spires, U. S. Navy (Retired). He greeted me warmly and we exchanged small talk. He was retiring from teaching, and I would be his successor – working with Master

Chief Richard Blaschuk, U. S. Navy (Retired). He educated me about the school mascot, The Trojan, and pointed at the large, brass emblem of 'The Trojan Head' right where we stood, directly outside of the NJROTC Classrooms. Next, he led me to the Conference Room in Principal Krystal Thomas' office, where she, Dr. Horak, and Lieutenant Commander Spires interviewed me.

Afterwards, he guided me on a tour of the school. Along the way, I noticed that on the walls high above the students' lockers were photos of previous Principals and notables who were either Alumni or Administrators, including Dr. Lenell Navarre, Superintendent; and Mrs. Rhona Israel, who was not only the Assistant Superintendent at the time, but my Soror (Delta Sigma Theta Sorority, Inc.). We continued on the tour and at one point, I heard my mother and father's voices speaking to me in unison saying, *"Stacy, stop right where you are."* I stopped. Then I heard, *"Look up."* I looked up. I was standing under a huge blue sign with white writing that read in big, bold letters: TIME AND PLACE. At that very moment, I knew this was a blessing that God had just for me. I whispered a tearful "Thank you" to my parents.

The next steps that I took along my journey led me *'From the Wardroom Into the Classroom.'* Dr. Stacy L. Henderson, Lieutenant, U. S. Navy (Retired) became the first African American and the first woman to hold the position as the Senior Naval Science

Instructor (SNSI) at Bloom Township High School in Chicago Heights, Illinois. The rest is history. *To God Be The Glory!*

Life presents us with a multitude of challenges, trials, and adversities; however, it also brings us much joy, happiness, and laughter. In everything we do it is always best to look to God for guidance. Proverbs 3:5-6 (KJV) charges us to *"Trust in the Lord with all thine heart; and lean not unto thine own understanding. In all thy ways acknowledge him and He shall direct thy path."*

There may be times when trusting God may seem difficult, however, it is indeed necessary. We do not know His ways, nor do we fully understand His methods. Hence, the importance of trusting that He is faithful and will keep His Word. Jeremiah 29:11 reminds us that God knows the plan, as such, we ought to trust the process. When we are in tune with Him, His instructions become very clear. Distractions oftentimes keep us from hearing God clearly. So, when struggling with difficult decisions, find a quiet place free of any distractions: telephones, television, noise – anything that can take your focus from hearing His voice. Pray honestly, seeking the way He would have you to go. Everything that He does is for our good.

STACY L. HENDERSON, PhD
Lieutenant, United States Navy (Retired)
Desert Shield, Desert Storm, Operation Enduring Freedom, Operation Iraqi Freedom, Operation New Dawn
(1991 – 2012)

Dr. Stacy L. Henderson, a native of Savannah, Georgia, is a retired Naval Officer with over 25 years of military service and experience. She is a Christian Educator, Inspirational Speaker, Businesswoman, and an International Best-Selling Author. She speaks four languages and has publications in more than 40 language translations - two of which are in the White House Library. Her *Stacy's Stocking Stuffers* Christmas Charity has provided toys, meals, coats, clothing and monetary support for families around the world since 1991. She has countless military and civilian accolades.

Stacy is a domestic abuse survivor turned advocate who shares her life experiences and relies on faith-based doctrines to motivate and inspire others to achieve their best mental, physical, and spiritual health. She is a Dean of Christian Leadership Schools at Christ Temple Baptist Church, Markham, Illinois and maintains close ties with her lifelong church family at Little Bryan Baptist Church, Savannah, Georgia. She has Degrees in Education, Health Services Management, Christian Leadership and Business Administration. A Proverbs 31 Woman, she utilizes her Spiritual Gifts to glorify God and edify His people. She is a loving wife, proud Mother of two adult children (KeiSha and William) and several bonus children, and a doting Grandmother – comprising a blessed and beautiful 'Blended and Extended' Family. To God be the Glory!

Contact information:
Dr. Stacy L. Henderson
P. O. Box 886913
Great Lakes, IL 60088

Dr. Stacy L. Henderson
240 Peachtree Street NW
#56850
Atlanta, Georgia 30343

Email – Drstacylhenderson@gmail.com
Instagram – @SLHenderson007

HE OUTRANKS THEM ALL

Leasia L. Brooks

Who knew that 26 years from then I would be calling myself an Air Force veteran? I had no intention of joining the military, and even when I did join my intent was not to enlist as active duty. But after talking to two of my high school classmates about their love for and experience in the Air Force, I decided to join. I enlisted in the United States Air Force on May 25, 1995, as a 3AX01 Information Manager (aka "the jack of all trades"). The journey throughout my career was not easy by far. I faced many obstacles and made many mistakes, but it is a decision that I do not regret.

My career started in Japan in 1995 and my career ended in Japan in 2008. During the first few months in Japan, I became a Christian. So now here I am in a foreign land learning how to live as an airman and a Christian. Thankfully, I had been assigned to a unit where my supervisor "just so happened" to be a Christian who not only served as my supervisor, but whether she realized it or not, a spiritual covering in the workplace. I faced many struggles during my first assignment, but God allowed my supervisor to dream and tell me things that were to come. I had two miscarriages. I suffered a mental breakdown and found myself in the mental ward on base after a Bible study gone wrong. I also suffered one of the worst heart breaks of my life, and later became pregnant and left Japan as a soon to be single mother. I thought those were some of the worst and most embarrassing times of my life, but it was just the beginning. After spending two years in Japan, I was reassigned to Florida.

Moving to Florida seemed to be just what the doctor ordered. At my first unit in Florida, I was the only junior airman in the Group and the unit took good care of me during my transition. One of the Non-Commissioned Officers (NCO) sacrificed her lunch breaks to help me search for a vehicle and apartment since I would soon have to move out of the dorms and off the base as I was a pregnant airman who could no longer live in the dorms. Another co-worker collected donations from fellow airmen to plan a baby shower and purchase items I would need for the baby and me. I lacked for nothing. There was so much provision that the staff was in awe. For every situation I faced from the fallout of Japan, God showed me love and never failed to provide a ram in the bush through co-workers, family, and friends. However, I still needed to grow as an airman and spiritually.

During that time frame, the Air Force decided to make major adjustments to the Information Management (IM) career field job duties. This change reduced the amount of Information Managers needed in the unit and basically pushed me out of a job in the Group. The Group decided to move me to one of their squadrons. Little did I know, the move to this squadron would be the beginning of what felt like the "valley of the shadow of death."

In this squadron, I was placed in the position of Non-Commissioned Officer in Charge (NCOIC), Information Management. This was the first time I was out on my own, in a one-deep position. Not as an airman but as an NCO with minimum military supervision to start up the IM office. There was no oversight or anyone in the squadron to groom or guide me as a new NCO. I shared office space with a civilian employee assigned to train and provide feedback. Because of the history of both of our fields being the "jack of all trades," my civilian counterpart was adamant about us not performing the traditional duties of a secretary. My duties in this position were to not only stand up the IM component of the unit but to establish several communications programs. I worked closely with outside agencies and their "auditors" to build and solidify programs within the unit. I was given project after project. Sadly, after a few years of being in the unit, things began to go downward quickly.

In 2004, I met my husband as he was assigned to complete one of the projects taking place in my unit. Some of the members of the squadron attended the wedding. Not long after, we were due to have our first son together. I began having pregnancy complications and was placed on half-days by the hospital staff, which did not go over too well with a few members in the unit. Eventually, I delivered and went on maternity leave. The unit decided to hire an Individualized Mobilization Augmentee (IMA) to fill my position while I was away. When I returned, I got a sense that something was off in the office. After some weeks had passed, the IMA revealed that the office turned against me while I was away. She relayed that they had given her a negative evaluation of my performance and had planned to "fire" me. She told me that she was a Christian believer and had decided to reserve making comments or passing judgment until she had observed me firsthand. Her evaluation was much different. She noticed that every time I began a project, they would hand me another project. Keep in mind, I am in a one-deep position. I believe that God had placed her there to not only to give me skillful insight on the multiple projects, but to alert me of the plans being formed by the civilian employee and senior management.

The climate in the office did not improve, it continued and got worse. I learned that the civilian employee tried to have my formal performance evaluation downgraded behind my back. Thankfully, my supervisor denied her request to lower my performance report due to a lack of supervisory feedback. In an effort to follow protocol, I decided to talk to the unit commander to resolve these and other mounting issues. However, when we met, he point-blank stared at me and began to praise the civilian employee and downplayed anything I had accomplished. Immediately I knew I could not trust my chain of command and informed him that I would prefer talking to Military Equal Opportunity (MEO) because I no longer had faith in my chain of command within the unit. He was not happy with my decision and at one point I was even told that I could not leave the office to see MEO because I was overwhelmed.

Eventually I found myself in mediation with the civilian employee and the MEO. God was still protecting me, but I was not mentally or spiritually prepared for what happened during the session. In the past, I have heard many people talk about being lied on and I could not say I had that experience until that particular MEO mediation. It was horrible. I was accused of not performing duties that the civilian employee and senior management agreed were not our area of responsibility. The accusation during the MEO mediation was a hard defense for me because traditionally it is not uncommon for Information Managers in other units to perform these duties I was being accused of not fulfilling. To be falsely accused was unreal to me, and to make matters worse, the entire office was willing to back her up on the lie, but MEO would not allow an ambush. The issue was not resolved. The only good thing that came out of the mediation was that it provided a voice for me.

Weeks passed after the mediation, and tensions were high in the office. It felt like a war had taken place. No one was talking in the office. I talked about what was going on and how I felt about the confusion in the office with my husband. His advice to dissipate the tension was as simple and practical as it comes. He told me *YOU* break the tensions in the room. *YOU* change the atmosphere. Regardless of their attitude and disposition, *YOU* go into the office and initiate conversation again. I took his advice and over the course of weeks, tensions began to drop, and friendly conversations began again. Although the atmosphere in the office changed, I was ready to leave. I had been in Florida for eight years. I wanted to go overseas with my husband and children or at the very least move to another unit on base. The squadron leaders told me that no one would "want me" because I was "hot" for a short tour. Without any orders and despite their words, I packed up my office space by faith; and within six months my husband and I received orders to Japan!

Although, I had a rough season in Japan the first assignment, I was sure that the second assignment would be perfect. This time I was married with children. But unfortunately, the first thing I had to face was residue from my assignment in Florida. The civilian employee had not been able to lower my performance evaluation while I was there, but somehow my Permanent Change of Station (PCS) evaluation had been lowered. Prior to this situation, I had not ever gotten less than the best rating on an evaluation. My new supervisor was furious and wanted to go battle. By this point I am mentally and spiritually drained. I don't want to fight. This was also the year that I missed being promoted by the number of points that the downgraded appraisal would have covered, had I not been downgraded.

Japan was my last assignment. By the time I reached the end of my career, the Wing staff had heard of everything I had endured throughout my career and offered me a position working at the highest level on base. I did not know it at the time, but God had been strategically placing and using supervisors, co-workers, and even strangers to love me, cover me, and grow me throughout my entire career. I do not regret my decision to join the Air Force. Neither do I hold any grudges. Those incidents caused me to feel and know the love of God, and to grow as an airman and Christian.

After I separated from the military, I continued to live in Japan for another couple of years under my spouse's orders. I pursued completing my undergraduate degree. I was told by a Department of Veteran Affairs representative that I could not reap the full benefits of using my Post 9/11 G.I. Bill, but *goodness* and *mercy* continued to follow me. A scholarship program was established for military spouses that happened to coincide with my educational pursuits, and I was able to continue my education at no cost. Later, I was hired by a federal government agency stateside prior to leaving Japan, where I received promotion after promotion! When I arrived, the agency informed me they had no plans of hiring me sight unseen through a telephone interview, but the interview went so well, they had no choice! Regardless of who or what system said "no," God always outranked them all!

I have since moved on. I am now able to serve others enduring hardships through counseling and ministry with compassion and love.

I attribute that first to God, in that He was always with me leading, protecting, and comforting me at every turn; then to "the excellence in all we do" ingrained in me by the Air Force, and finally all of the trials throughout my career that caused professional and spiritual growth that strengthened me to live both in the boots, and beyond the boots.

LEASIA L. BROOKS, TSgt (Separated)
United States Air Force
*Operation Noble Eagle, Operation Enduring Freedom,
Operation Iraqi Freedom*
(1995 – 2008)

Leasia Brooks is a native of Talladega, Alabama. She holds a BS in Management Studies from the University of Maryland University College and a MA in Mental Health Counseling from Bowie State University. Leasia served in the United States Air Force as an Information Manager and Knowledge Operator. During her thirteen years in the Air Force, she served as Non-Commissioned Officer in Charge in several stateside and overseas units, including a joint service unit in Afghanistan.

Leasia is also a published author of three literary works, *Who Wants to Talk to God? Let's Chat, It's Not That Hard, A 21-Day Devotional,* and *¿Quién quiere hablar con Dios?*

Leasia's mission is to teach strategies to help individuals and families learn how to create an environment to live in peace; experience spiritual growth and have healthier relationships. She has worked in ministry with individuals and families for over 20 years and enjoys helping others succeed.

As a professional, she serves as a Mental Health Therapist in the state of Maryland. She is a certified Prepare-Enrich Marriage Facilitator assisting couples worldwide in learning and implementing healthy skills to thrive both individually and collectively as they grow in love. Leasia is also a Certified National Anger Management Specialist and is pursuing specialized certification for treating trauma survivors.

Leasia currently resides in Prince George's County, Maryland with her husband, José, and their children.

I Am A Resilient Warrior

Katriana R. Walker

For I know the plans and thoughts that I have for you, Katriana says the LORD, plans for peace and well-being and not for disaster, to give you, Katriana a future and a hope.
(Jeremiah 29:11, Amplified Bible)

I knew at a very young age that I was different, but I was told I was a happy baby. See, I wasn't supposed to be here today. I was supposed to be aborted, but my birth mother carried me to term, and placed me up for adoption. I was adopted at 6-months by a couple who were unable to have children if their own.

I distinctly remember at a very young age thinking something was wrong with me because I never fit in. I was never a part of the families I was assigned to for that season of my life. As I grew up, I was very active in various activities, but even with all I had going on, I always found myself standing on the outside looking in, and now, I understand why. I was not created to fit in, but I am a peculiar person, a royal priesthood, anointed and set apart for my Father's use (1 Peter 2:9).

My daddy was very authentic, kind, honest, transparent, loving, and generous, always reminding me how much he loved me, but he worked so much. However, my mother was quite the opposite. She was very strict, and one dimensional when it came to me, and our relationship. As I was growing up, she was my best friend, but as I began to get older that suddenly changed and at the age of 16, I found myself out on the streets with no place to live, kicked out of the only place I had ever called home

You see, the young lady you just read about was an alcoholic at the age of 12 because she had been touched, molested, and even raped. I've always felt afraid, terrified, anxious, and that my life wasn't worth living, but I was afraid to die. So, I would drink, drink, and drink to numb the pain and the reality of what my life had become – a mental and emotional prison that kept me bound well beyond my childhood.

I vividly recall getting on my knees, and even laying in my bed praying, crying out to the Lord, asking Him to help me, but there was no relief for my pain. I didn't know how to process what I had gone through and endured at the hands of those who were chosen and supposed to love me but instead chosen to abuse me mentally, physically, emotionally, and sexually.

I didn't understand the Lord's plans for my life, so I chose to drink, rebel, self-isolate, and withdraw from the cares of this world inside of a bottle (which caused suicidal ideations and a multiplicity of suicidal attempts). It's because of this pain, I began to search for love in anything and anyone I could find who remotely showed an interest in me. Slowly, I began to spiral down into a dark place, not truly comprehending and understanding how to process the multiple crises, traumas, disappointments, deception, manipulation, pain, confusion, rejection, self-rejection, bitterness, and insecurities I'd dealt with at that point in my life.

The enemy did everything he could to me as a child to keep me from getting into position and in a place of knowing who I was and Whose I was. It was through domestic violence, sexual abuse, and multiple rapes that I knew there had to be more to life than what I was experiencing. Of course, I didn't know any of this at the time, and because I came into agreement with those thoughts, they consumed and invaded every area of my life. I had given Satan and his kingdom direct legal access to me and into my life.

I surrendered and gave my life to Lord at 16-years old and joined the Arkansas Army National Guard (ARNG) at 17-years old as an Administrative Specialist. I attended Basic Training during the summer of my junior and senior years and my Advanced Individual Training (AIT) at Fort Jackson, South Carolina two days after graduating (which I almost didn't do, because I had missed so many days of school because I was displaced and homeless). After I returned from training, I switched from the ARNG to active-duty Army.

After going active duty, my whole world changed, and my life was never the same. My first few years were a bit tumultuous because I didn't understand what was really expected of me but once I did, it was on active duty that the Lord blessed tremendously. I literally ran through the ranks, and intentionally took assignments that others would shy away from to set myself apart from others within my job specialty.

It worked, and I received a call from my branch at Department of the Army. I had just volunteered to deploy, and they asked me if I'd be interested in a new assignment deploying into one of our theaters of operation. They explained to me no one had done the assignment before, and I'd be the first female to do it if I agreed to go. I immediately, said 'yes,' then they began to give me the few details they had about the assignment which was training the that countries Army.

It took over a year for the details of the assignment to come together, by then I assisted with setting up the assignment, the orders, and what we'd do to train and prepare others who received the same assignment. We were Military Transition Teams (MiTT), which were 10-man teams who would be embedded with the Iraqi Army to train them on various aspects of standing up their own army and taking their country back from that country's enemies.

Our team was assigned to Multi-National Forces – MNSTC-I for augmentees, mission and intelligence support. We were later assigned to one of the Brigades to train and we were a Motor Transportation Regiment (MTR) training on finance, casualty assistance, basic administrative duties, combat medical operations, and convoy operations. We had more than 900 soldiers, officers, and commanders to train and ensure they understood each aspect that we were assigned to teach them.

I personally worked with several government agencies to include the Ministry of Finance, Ministry of Interior, Ministry of Defense, and Ministry of Human Rights. These branches assisted me in teaching their Army how to conduct payday activities, personnel files, casualty reports, the payout of death benefits.

With the type of assignment we had, our teams were allowed to conduct convoys even when the remainder of the country was not because the roads were either red or black. It was on this assignment I met the Lord in a new way during a convoy as Convoy Commander. The sun was starting to go down and our vehicles were being released to us from the maintenance shop. We were heading out back to our combat outpost (COP) overlooking the city, when I realized all the roads were locked (red and black) and we received a report of imminent danger heading into the town we had to pass through to get to the COP.

Everyone was screaming through the headsets at me, "what are we going to do, we have to get out of here before it gets dark." I heard it but I didn't; I was terrified, and it was at that moment I began to realize I had the life of my soldiers and comrades in my hands as I made the decision, that I couldn't make (they always tell us, we train in peacetime for war so that it becomes second nature – without having to think about it, but that's not true because the human factor and the verisimilitude of death isn't in play when we are training). I suddenly heard my gunner say, "Master Sergeant what are we going to do? We gotta move!"

It felt like a few minutes had passed but, it was only a few seconds, everything slowed down and I began to panic on the inside. I remember thinking about those people I'd seen as we traveled throughout Iraq as we passed them on the road and would later get a report they were attacked. I didn't want us to be one of them, I didn't want anyone knocking on my parents' door telling them they were sorry.

At that moment, all I could do was cry out in my desperation to God, and I said, "Lord help me!" An instantly, I had a sliver of peace and told everyone 'Let's go!' As we entered the town, there were people everywhere and cars all on the side of the roads. It was terrifying because this would be the place to hit us, because they were all over the road and we couldn't pass. But even as we stopped, I remembered the Lord, and said, "Lord please," and I raised my hand to point this way to my driver and I realized I was shaking, but we began to move and didn't stop until we got back to the COP.

We made it back by the grace of God and as we made it into the gate the tears began to fall, and I was terrified. I sat there as everyone got out and began to download the vehicles and prepare for the back-brief, but all I could do was sit there. It took me a while to get out because my legs felt as if they weren't going to sustain me. I didn't make it to the briefs. I couldn't come out of my room, and I couldn't stop crying. I also realized at the time that I honestly had no idea why I was there; but if I wanted to make it out of this place alive, I was going to have to trust the Lord like never before.

I was traumatized and couldn't sleep for days after this; and the days turned to weeks, months, and years. I suffered in silence for many years in a broken and distorted paradigm of deep levels of fear, terror and torment which gripped my heart every day of my life for as long as I could remember. And believe it or not, suicidal ideations – unbeknownst to me – became my drug of choice when alcohol and sex wouldn't do it anymore. Honestly, I lost my mind amidst all I had endured, but God was faithful to me, and He gave it [my mind] back.

It all came to a head a few years later in 2019 as I was on my knees in my hallway crying out to the Lord with my 9mm locked and loaded ready to end the pain that had consumed my life. I cried out to the Lord and said, "If You're real, I need You to show up and help me… I need You, Lord, I need You!" And let me tell you, as I laid my head on my lap and held the weapon up, I felt the Lord's embrace and I dropped my 9mm and rolled over on my side and just cried for hours as the Lord comforted me and held me in His arms. My life was never the same and a few months later, I gave my life back to Christ because I realized life wasn't worth living without Him.

I wish I could tell you that everything was good from there, but it wasn't. My whole life fell apart and it was in this place I learned how to pray, war, worship and get into the presence of the Lord. I learned to lean and depend on the Lord and not people, because no matter what happened the Lord would never leave me nor forsake me (Deuteronomy 31:6). I cried for years, then one day I had stopped crying and started to wage war with the devil and his cohorts. The Lord has taught me how to use the Word as a weapon of war. He built me up and fortified me in the fire and for His glory. It was in this place that a *resilient warrior* was born and out of the ashes she arose. I am a Resilient Warrior!

A Resilient Warrior who the Lord called to step out of the darkness that engulfed her into His marvelous light, and into His unwavering love, and in doing so I was clothed in His glory (1 Peter 2:9 *paraphrased for emphasis*). I then picked up my sword and began to war for those who couldn't war for themselves. I later learned how to trust the Lord pass what I could see and understand, into a place of knowing that no matter what I faced I wouldn't face it alone. Despite what it looked like, smelt like, and sounded like it was going to work out for my good because I loved Him, and I am called according to His purpose in Christ Jesus (Romans 8:28).

The Lord has taught and is teaching me how to convert my military training and combat readiness into practical everyday prayer targets to take out the enemy and his kingdom. You see, I wasn't created to fit in; I was created to be an ambassador, trailblazer, forerunner, and warrior for Christ Jesus. I am chosen, a descendant of Jesus' bloodline and of a royal priesthood. I am a holy vessel, and admittedly a peculiar person who glorifies God and gives Him all the praises, and honor due His name for the work He has done in and through me for His glory.

Its time **arise resilient warrior** and take back everything that's been stolen from you and your bloodline in Jesus' name. If He, did it for me, He will do it for you, resilient one. *"Blessed be the LORD my strength, which teacheth my hands to war, and my fingers to fight"* (Psalm 144:1).

KATRIANA R. WALKER, First Sergeant (Ret.)
United States Army
*Operation Enduring Freedom, Operation Iraqi Freedom,
Operation New Dawn*
(1992 – 2013)

Katriana R. Walker is a disabled veteran who served as an Operations Noncommissioned Officer (NCO), Administrative Specialist, Recruiter, Security Manager / Officer, Operations Manager, Drill Sergeant, Advanced NCO Instructor, one of the first females to conduct the Military Transition Team (MiTT) / Combat Advisor mission to the MNSTC-I mission, Project Manager, First Sergeant, Senior Human Resource Manager, and Senior Enlisted Advisor (SEA) Joint Military Postal Activity – Pacific Command (JMPA-PAC).

She's a survivor of molestation, rape, and domestic violence, educator, coach & consultant, trainer, mentor, speaker, Doctoral Candidate, Prayer and Worship Warrior, and Prophet who operates with an Apostolic Grace. She's an aspiring author who will publish her first book in the Winter of 2021, *I Am, Because He Is*.

She's anointed to come alongside those who've been hurt, abandoned, rejected, misunderstood and in pain from the weight of various psychological traumas of life. She's called to the nations, and desire is to see God's will be done in the earth and people saved, delivered, healed, set free, healthy, and whole in every area of their life by love of God. She is a servant at heart who loves to see Christ at work in the lives of unbelievers, backsliders, and those who find themselves in a prodigal situation being restored through the love and blood of Jesus. Katriana's ministry and business can be experienced through Facebook and Instagram.

Facebook: Resiliency Is Me
IG: Resilient_Warrior_Official

Businesses:
Resiliency Is Me Coaching & Consulting
Resilient Warrior Academy

It Was All Good...Until

Ossawa F. Gillespie

Early in my Air Force career, I found myself filling out the family separation form after being activated and skipping the section for dual military household. Thinking even though my girlfriend was also military we both would be out and not having to navigate those trials of a dual military household. That was early in the Operation Enduring Freedom mission, and most would not have thought that this war would be extended so soon in my years of service. Several years later, I found myself in that situation – A dual military household with my wife, an Army reservist attending her Unit Training Assemblies (UTAs) one weekend each month and me an Air Force reservist going on and off orders with three kids.

The first three years of my marriage, I was the only one being activated and spending my time about two hours away from home. I drove home most weekends and sometimes during my work week to spend time with the family. My wife still had her monthly obligation of one weekend a month to the Army Reserve. Often a family member or friend would have to watch our kids for a day or so. Both of us being in our mid-twenties, life was fast-paced and required a lot of coordination getting kids to their daycare and our obligation to the U.S military left little time for just the two of us. It became a life of routine with time management to fulfill all our responsibilities.

Summer of 2008 I was finally coming off orders and would be able to spend more time home. My wife was ecstatic because we had a newborn and enjoyed more time waking up in the same bed. Those emotions were short lived when my wife would be getting the calls to be activated and returning to Iraq for a second tour. Over those next months the preparation had begun for the roles to be reversed. I was home with the kids, and she was gone for 6-months, only being available through Skype. As a mother, she went through an array of emotions realizing she would miss her youngest child's first birthday. She wondered if her daughter would even recognize her when returned. Unlike me during my activation orders, I was still able to return home often because I was stationed only two hours away. When the day came for my wife to leave, just like most families seeing their loved ones leaving for military duty, a piece of our family left from our household.

There I stood with a four-year-old, a two-year-old, and a six-month-old saying all the necessary things to assure her that we will be fine... *"We are good"* ... *"We got this"* ... *"Don't worry; we have friends ready to help"* and all the while anxiety was creeping up because it's all me now. Those little faces needed me to help them understand where mom was going, and that life was fine. The grind began counting down the days until that piece of us would return and make our family whole again. The kids and I soon began a routine that felt like survival to handle all the responsibilities. Single dad mode was in full swing, and everything had to be done at a certain time to achieve goals. Morning, evening, and night routines had to be established because I didn't want to miss a thing. There were countless routines to maintain the household but sure enough there were things that would derail the household.

Anytime mom (my wife) would try to call on Skype, the family didn't care about the routine. We all missed her and would rather spend our time seeing her. Our middle child – with her smile seeing her mother on the computer – always assured me that we were ok. Their mom was so creative to continue the connection with the kids being over 6,000 miles away. She mailed books with a thumb drive of her reading them so they could easily hear her voice going to bed. These were gifts she thought we would enjoy that would help us with counting those days down. Even though the family was unable to touch or embrace her for those warm hugs only mothers know how to give, we knew that piece of us wasn't gone because we always felt her in our hearts.

There was this one day that has been seared in my mind because I was pushed to that point as a father trying to maintain. This day started out as many of the other days rushing to get the kids to the daycare…Changing diapers, getting them dressed, making sure everyone ate because we had to be there when the daycare doors opened on base. By then, we had things down to a science even with dealing with backed-up traffic at the gate to get on base for daycare. During this time, my civilian job was working with Alban CAT as a technician for generators. This job required me to drive everywhere in the Maryland, Virginia, and District of Columbia area. After dropping off the kids, I was off maneuvering through traffic to get to my company vehicle to be on the customer site to inspect their generators.

This day I was driving to a site 40-miles away from where I picked up my company vehicle in Virginia. Things were going good until midday when I just felt like something was in my throat. I just kept pushing because I had to get back to my car and pick up my little ones. As the day went on, I could just feel my health declining. This was turning into one of the toughest days I experienced during my wife's deployment. I picked up the kids and made it home, but by this time my body was aching, and my throat felt closed off. There was nothing but pain when I swallowed, and it seemed like I produced even more spit than usual causing me to swallow even more. Dinner had to be made and I was one of those people that did not like to inconvenience family or friends, so I kept pushing on. It was a chicken nugget and fries day because my energy level was tapping out. As the sun was going down, so was I... right in the kid's doorway. I just laid in the doorway of their room. They still wanted to play, and I was in that light sleep to make sure I just had them contained in the room.

My mother just so happened to be doing one of those calls checking up on us. My mom knew her child. She said she could just hear it in my voice when I answered. Nana mode was activated within moments. She was heading over to get the kids and telling me to get myself over to the doctor. Before I knew it, she was at my door walking in and packing bags to take the kids over to her place. During this time, I was just sitting there because I was truly exhausted. I agreed with my mother and decided that I would head over to the doctor in the morning. I couldn't even tell you if I was asleep before or after they left. I tried to drink some cold medicine to see if that would help at some point in the middle of the night.

That morning, I called off work and headed over to the doctor. My body was not as sore, but my throat still felt closed and hard to swallow. Sure enough, the doctor just knew I had strep throat and a test proved him right. I was given those penicillin pills and I wondered how was I supposed to swallow those knowing I could barely get down liquid? My mother already knew she was going to keep the kids for a few days until I got better. I couldn't be even more thankful. Later that evening I heard the computer ringing. It was Skype and I was explaining the last 24-hours to my wife. I could see all the emotions coming over her as I knew she wanted to be there for me and the kids. I think that was one of the moments that added to why my wife got out after that second deployment. We had two months remaining and I and the kids were very much looking forward to this tour to being over.

When she returned, I could see it as if it were yesterday, even though it was well over a decade ago. The whole family packed in the car ready to pick her up from Baltimore/Washington International airport. The excitement of just waiting and looking to see her face in person – not on a screen. I let the kids go greet their mom first. I was not prepared for my youngest daughter's reaction, but I did understand. The last time she saw her mom she wasn't even walking. When her mom picked her up, she burst out crying. As the strong soldier she was, she was just glad to be home and able to reconnect any lost ties with the family.

My wife soon got out of the Army and her new MOS (military occupational specialty) became being there and supporting the family. I've been amazed at all the dedication she has put into the family since then. I separated from the Air Force four years later, but our time in the service has strengthened our family because we cherish the moments when we are together even more. Those days were not the easiest being young with young kids. Since my wife has returned, I don't believe I have been that sick since. She must be doing all the right things.

OSSAWA F. GILLESPIE, TSgt (Separated)
United States Air Force Reserves
(2001 – 2015)

Ossawa F. Gillespie joined the Air Force Reserves May 2001 as an electric and environmental specialist. As his career progressed, he became a flying crew chief on the Galaxy C-5. Soon after September 11, 2001, many reservists were activated, which ended his college career at Morgan State University. Ossawa spent several years on and off active-duty orders getting planes fixed to fly missions during Operation Iraqi Freedom and Operation Enduring Freedom. As a flying crew chief, he was set on many missions – delivering and picking up payloads for the Air Force under Operation Noble Eagle.

Ossawa's career was cut short after fourteen years due to an off-duty accident that left his arm partially disabled. Returning to school, Ossawa completed his Bachelor of Arts in Psychology from Hawaii Pacific University and continued his graduate degree studies in Counseling Psychology at Bowie State University. Ossawa now invests his time in training to become a counselor specializing in the military community. Ossawa Gillespie is a dedicated husband, father, brother, uncle, and son to his family. He spends his life living towards God's plan.

LIVING IN THE DARK WITH PTS

Curtis "Gunny" Jones

"Tell my wife I love her!" My soul will never be quiet. How do I describe the post-traumatic stress monster within me without reliving the pain, anxiety, and rage of who I have become? Where do I start? I was 18-years old, an active-duty Radioman in the United States Marine Corps, when this monster first injured my soul and began to mold me into a walking hand grenade ready to go off.

Fellow Marines and I were participating in a simulated assault combined arms operation – air, artillery, and mortars. I can see the mortarmen – highly trained Marines and the best of the active-duty Armed Forces showing off its might and power in the face of indisputable danger and death. Everything was going well until we got a call over the radio that there was a "short round," which meant that no one knew where it would land. Adrenaline high, all mental, emotional, and physical responses at the "ready" the round landed 500 meters (about twice the height of the Empire State Building) from my position. The expert creator of post-traumatic stress was about the distance of 11 school buses lined up from front to rear or a mere 6-minute walk, or five one-hundred-foot garden hoses laid male to female, end-to-end from me and men I had come to know as brothers. During that same training exercise, we lost an aircraft. I was talking on the radio to the pilot when he lost hydraulics and control of his plane, and he crashed into a mountain. The sight and sound of that plane hopelessly headed for that mountain – the pilot unable to climb, unable to land, and the immovable – is permanently helplessly entrenched on my mind, heart, and soul. The last words he said were, "tell my wife I love her!" My soul can never be quiet! Memories of the smell, sight, sound, and touch of death, danger, and the constant "ready" lives with me – forever.

After I left that unit, I was assigned to another unit. I was still a radio operator, but this time, I was flying on a Ch46 helicopter. I was the mail clerk for my unit, and part of the unit was in the field on another island. It was my job to get them their mail. Receiving mail is one of the highlights of active-duty members especially if you are on a field exercise. I hopped a ride on the next bird going to the field. I delivered the mail, and we were headed back when the 46 started having problems. The crew chief started throwing gear and other essentials out of the bird to lighten the load, but that was not helping. I knew we were going down! I prayed, "Lord, get me out of this and I'll go back to church!" We had lost an engine and were falling out of the sky! All I could do was continue to pray and remember my training about what to do if I ever went down in the water. I was scared. Here I am at 19-years old facing death one more time! We regain the second engine minutes before we hit the water. We ended up doing what I later found out what was called a "water taxite." Yes, from that day on I have been going to Church! Learning about Life.

Fast forward two years, I am on deployment with an artillery unit. We were assigned to support a rifle battalion. As a forward observer (FO), it is my job to call in the fire mission. I was an outstanding FO and I loved putting steel on target. I can still remember some of the fire missions to this day, "A2E this is X3E fire mission over, X3E this is A2E fire mission roger, 2E this 3X troops in the open request HE and WP in effect, roger HE and WP in effect shot out, shot over rounds on target fire for effect!" Yes, I must say that I did love what I did, until one day when I was walking down the street and I had an eye-opening dream during the day that I had taken so many lives in the blink of an eye! Unless you have done it and seen the carnage that artillery rounds can do to the human body, you cannot believe it. It is one thing to go to the movies or watch TV, but to see it firsthand, to live it…to be it… is a different world. The scenes will never leave your mind.

From day one in Boot, we are trained to kill the enemy, but you do not think that he or she will be within 10-yards of you. During another mission in another country, I was going out to set up a night ambush sight. When we were doing the recon for the site, an enemy soldier came into view. At this time, I raised my weapon, took aim, shot, and killed the soldier. I hit him in the upper body with two rounds from my Remington Model-870 12-gauge shotgun that I was issued! I will never forget that day, or the look in his eyes as I fired my weapon. It was a ridiculously sweltering day, and we were doing what Marines do on a patrol when we think nothing is going to happen, laughing, and joking. The other Marines with me could not believe what just happened; their Sergeant just killed a man who would have killed all of us if he could. After it was all said and done, we continued with our mission and returned to base. A report was filed and that was the end of that. This is just one of the many faces of Ghosts that live within me – day and night.

I can also recall the two times when I was interrogated. The first time I was going on leave in a country that was supposed to be welcoming to Americans. I got off the plane and the next thing I knew, I was asked *was I a Marine* and I answered, "yes." I was then taken by gunpoint into an office and questioned about the place I was stationed. I was questioned for over an hour until the U.S. Embassy got there! The thing that I remember most about that day and still today is Article I of The Code of Conduct, "I am an American fighting man (Marine). I serve in the Forces which guard our country and our way of life. I am prepared to give my life in its defense." To this day I still do not know why I was singled out for questioning. I reported everything that took place to the Intelligence officer upon my return. That took place in 1985.

The second time was in 1995 when I and another Marine were assigned to transport equipment to a ship that was docked in an overseas port. Once we arrived in country at the airport, we were confronted by the military and ordered to open our cases, which I refused to do. During this trip, I was under orders to transport classified equipment and documents to the Marines on board the ship. This action caused a standoff and weapons came out on both sides. Things cooled down once the U.S. Embassy people arrived. If the Embassy personal would have been on time and met us at the plane like we were told, everything would have worked out okay in the first place!

In another country, myself and a group of my Marines went out to a club one night. There had been intelligence reports of terrorists targeting clubs that Americans visited. We were the only Americans in the club during the time. As time went on more people started entering the club; one guy walked in the place that just did not look right to me. After a closer look at the man, I realized that he had a grenade. I took the necessary action I had to and got my Marines together and got them the hell out of there! That is why today I do not like going places and do not feel comfortable 90% of the time around a large group of people!

I have had many challenges in my 21 years in the Marines: Two helicopter crashes; being on a plane that was shot at by a Service to Air Missile (S.A.M.); I ran over a landmine, missed a tripwire; and I was shot in the chest, but my vest took the round. As a result of my close encounters with death and danger – mine and others…friends and foe – I have not only suffered injuries of the mind, but those of the body as well.

The worst thing I can think of that still haunts me to this day is taking the life of a woman and a child. I can still see them in my mind's eye as if it happened yesterday. On a dreadful day I can hear myself telling her not to come any closer, but she just would not stop coming! I aimed my 9mm pistol at her and a baby in her arms, still yelling for her to stop! She does not stop, so I fire the shot that stops her forward motion forever. How was I supposed to know she was carrying a real child and not an IED? I did my job and that is what the Head Doctor (psychologist) at the VA Medical Center told me, too! Not that the other things that I have done for love of country are less damning! My soul refuses to be quiet and there are times when my soul is so sad!

My service to this Nation and its people has my moral compass so screwed up it hurts to be me! Yes, I have talked to my Pastor, but most preachers will never understand the hell we Veterans live with day-to-day and will died with! At the end of the day, I would do it all over again. Most people would say I must be crazy to want to go through all that hell again! My answer to that would be, "If not me, then who?" Yet, I am still here living everyday with PTS (Post-Traumatic Stress). because I am in it to win it. I fight every day to keep the demons at bay! For I will win my battle with PTS. Like I said, "I'm in it to win it!"

After I retired from the Marines, I went to work for the FBI during that time, which was a 10-year hitch. That's right, I just could not get away from serving my country. People always want to know what I did there. I am only going to tell what I can. I worked the crash site of United Flight 93. I raised the flag that flew over the Nation's Capital there on September 13, 2001. From Pennsylvania, I went to New York City and worked the site of the Twin Towers. I spent time in GTMO Bay Cuba working on and off for a year. I also worked the DC Sniper mission among other unfortunate things that were happening in our country. I then went on to work for the DoD for another 9-years until my legs gave out one day, which lead to the first of many surgeries that all came from my time on active duty! So, now I have set my sights to helping every Veteran that I can…helping them to live a better life. Not to leave you hanging – I did regain the use of my legs!

Living with PTS has become a living hell, yet I live! I have an OUTSTANDING support system – family that loves me, and a wife that keeps me on point. I talk to other vets, and I use the VA. I am here to let you know you, too, can make it. Yes, we have lost many of our brothers and sisters to this demon I call PTS, but this Marine Gunny is "In it to Win it!"

CURTIS "GUNNY" JONES, Gunner Sergeant (Ret.)
United States Marine Corps
(1977 – 1998)

Curtis D. Jones is a veteran. He served tours in the Gulf, Haiti, Bosnia, and other parts of the world. He worked on the United Airlines Flight 93 crash site in rural Pennsylvania and the Twin Towers. He has received the Defense Meritorious Medal and many other awards. Curtis has also worked in security, communications and electronic warfare and has experience with the Combined Joint Task Force and the FBI. He is trained in Anti-Terrorism and Contingency of Emergency Operations.

Since his retirement, Curtis helps veterans by volunteering with various organizations, such as the Veterans of Foreign Wars, Fleet Reserve Association, Disabled American Veterans, NABVETS,

AMVETS and he is the Commander of American Legion Cook-Pinkney Post 141. He is involved with the NAACP for Anne Arundel County, Veterans Affairs Commission for Anne Arundel County, the Chesapeake Veterans Alliance, and the National Veterans Intermediary.

Curtis is a native of Philadelphia. He is a husband, father, and grandfather. He resides in Anne Arundel County, Maryland.

MENTAL MADNESS

Raphael J. Holmes

Using your imagination during your childhood was one of the best gifts given to us. We would sit around and dream about what we wanted to be when we grew up; the celebrity we wanted to meet or claimed to marry one day; or even our dream house with our dream car(s) in the multi-car garage. The same mansions we used to watch on MTV Cribs, yeah? Not quite? Never mind that. We would often dream or imagine ourselves as a doctor, traveling musician, a professional athlete, or even an athletic trainer for the NFL. Either way, we allowed ourselves multiple opportunities to use our imagination and its captivating ability to envision much of what we considered our goals and aspirations.

For me, I would never imagine or think about my goals and aspirations being a time where my imagination would see other visions beyond my control. Never would I imagine my goals and aspirations being a time where I would question or argue with my own mind. It sounds wicked thinking that you would argue with your own mind, but you can. What if my mind had an opportunity to square up and fight me? Who would win? Sounds like a war worth watching. I mean, having the ability to totally control the being you empower in a manner beyond control makes the imagination more intriguing – or does it become frightening? I would vote frightening because doesn't your mind understand the control it has over you? Do you understand the control you have over your mind? Or does mind over matter immediately kick in? The unfortunate answer to those questions varies, depending on the individual and their circumstances. But being frightened by these dreams, or mental tug of wars, appears to be the new norm. Oh well, just deal with it. But that's not quite the answer we're looking for, is it?

Some high school graduates dream of joining the military after graduating from high school. In some cases, the decision to serve in the military is generally influenced by someone in their family – often a parent, grandparent, or another family member. Then you have those that choose to join because they didn't want to go to college, but somehow became a full-time graduate student. That seems a bit insane, doesn't it?! Regardless of their reasoning, their aim is to serve and to serve their country with pride and dignity. In the military you would be awarded opportunities to experience life that you wouldn't otherwise have been able to experience. Traveling to countries you never thought or knew existed. You hear about various countries on TV, but not much about the ones most military members visit for a four-, six-, or even 12-month deployment. Deployments introduced you to a culture and environment you wouldn't experience anywhere back at home. The food was amazing (that's subjective, depending on the branch), the tax breaks were wonderful, the cultures were life-altering to learn about, and the HR (Human Remains) ceremonies for the fallen.

The fallen! It's never a pleasant feeling hearing about a brother or sister in arms who's no longer with us. The pain and mental torture become much more intense when you hear of those who took an altered path and matters into their own hands. These circumstances cut deep, but much deeper when it's someone you know. Very similar to how cops feel when they lose one of their own who wore the same uniform. You then wonder if you knew something was wrong. Whether or not they sent you a cry for help and you missed or ignored the signs and clues. Did someone send out a smoke signal? SOS, abort mission! The constant questions and returning spiral of mind games, or the mental exhaustion of questions you may never get the answers to.

Where were you when your wingman needed you most? Ugh, here is when the guilt kicks in and starts beating you to a pulp. Why didn't you do more? Why couldn't you be there to save them? Truth of the matter is, there may not have been a single thing you could have done differently. But how do you tell your mind that? Convincing yourself should be a breeze, hopefully. However, it won't let you live this down. Not only are you torturing yourself mentally, but then the emotional torture becomes the newer and bigger battle. Don't worry, just cry yourself to sleep and it'll be all over in the morning. Remember, trouble don't last always. This seems like a joke when your mind is going mad over situations beyond your control. There's no way you could've known that your brother or sister in arms wouldn't return home from their deployment. There was no way you would've known that your battle buddy wouldn't return to post after going home on leave/vacation. So why does your mind lead you to believe otherwise? It's easier to tell yourself to get over it, but how does one truly get over it? The constant lingering in your mind doesn't help. Nor does it provide an avenue for mental rest and relaxation. Now ask your distant but close cousin, PTSD (Post-Traumatic Stress Disorder), do you mind giving us a break now? No?

As adults we may wish we could travel back in time. Back to when we had absolutely no cares in the world. Send us back to the time where we didn't have bills and life was grand. Send us back to the time where we were our brother or sister's keeper. Return us to that last phone call or text message so we can converse with them again. Going a step further, take us back to the time before we left for a specific deployment and PTSD became a distant cousin we struggle to disown. Yeah, that's it! Find us a time machine, please and thank you. Wouldn't life be much easier with time machines? We would never have to face the reminders of the traumas we experienced. Physical control over the mind at its finest. Mind over matter in its truest and pure, yet rare, form.

Like most people do with their family, you fuss and fight. This adopted cousin we never asked for, PTSD, will take every ounce of strength and motivation away from you. Rather draining to be honest. PTSD often serves as a reminder of a, or numerous, traumatic experiences. One constant reminder comes in the form of dreams. Often, they're more of a nightmare than a dream. Most dreams tell a story, some more peaceful and memorable than others. Waking up in the middle of the night from nightmares is generally what all of mankind experiences. However, the night sweats, tears on your pillow, and overall panic attacks are more reasons to be frightened. We may watch a scary movie at night and coincidentally, we have a nightmare where we're reliving the movie. This time you're one of the main characters running for your life and trying to find your safe place, to refrain from being attacked, hurt, or killed. But what happens when the nightmare is filled with you reliving the experience you once had? Picture it, Sicily 1932. Disregard; bad timing.

Fighting a constant war in your mind is nerve-racking. Have you ever sat around in the corner of your room wondering why the room was caving in and you know it's rather impossible? Have you ever tried to get a decent night's rest and you're having a severe anxiety attack in your sleep? That's insane, right?! Having an anxiety attack in your sleep introduces you to a war you would never imagine as a teenager, or even as an adult. You constantly run through scenarios in your head wondering where it stems from. Or worse, you replay the various traumas over and over in your head, as if you're able to produce a changed outcome. Reality hits and you realize the outcome never changes, and you're still stuck in the cage with the same repeated traumas tormenting you. Then the ultimate question becomes, "Why is this happening to me?" Would you be crazy if you asked yourself 'Why not me?' I'd dare not say that makes it acceptable. Certainly not if those same nightmares are being relived and you're waking up to a puddle of tears or sweat on your pillow. The madness with nightmares comes when you're staying awake all night watching TV because you can't sleep. Insomnia is at its peak, the medication is no longer working, and you're just up with your thoughts. You stop paying attention to the movie, or TV show you were watching because it's no longer a distraction. Better yet, now your thoughts are overwhelming and have taken over. There it is, AGAIN! Your thoughts have once again come in like a rushing wind and consumed you to no end.

Joining the military was already a major game changer. The steady paychecks on the 1st and the 15th, the health and education benefits, and even the military discounts added up when you're shopping or eating out. The ultimate game changer for most comes with PTSD and everything surrounding it. PTSD creates your own personal hell as a constant reminder that it should've been you. Let us not think ahead and realize there's life to live after departing from the military. Adapting to life after the military is extremely challenging. Many people struggle with being able to physically and mentally relieve themselves of the familiar, or the safety net called the military. Now there's another anxiety trigger because what is familiar to us is now coming to an end. But somehow it never feels like an ending. Your peace and mental freedom still never arrive, and what continues to remain are the mental hurricanes.

The more your anxiety triggers, the mental war becomes more petrifying. As advised, you seek therapy in hopes of therapy becoming your new saving grace. Therapy is not a bad idea. Now you have an outlet and someone, without judgement, to speak with about your traumas. Of course, they're going to be able to tell me I'm not crazy and it's just a mind game. Evidently my mind becomes free, and you begin to feel normal again. At this point, what does normal feel like? Will you ever be normal again? Someone once said, "You'll never be normal once you serve in the military." Although that could be true in some instances, I refuse to accept that because normal will never be normal for again. The new normal starts with the coping mechanisms you learn in therapy, as well as, when you start to live life after leaving the military. But don't worry, your mind has packed several suitcases of tumultuous thoughts to haunt you wherever you go…or so it seems.

Moving forward in life, one can only hope and pray that times get better. But at the same time, you may wonder how might 'better' truly look for you. Does that mean the nightmares finally go away? Will the mental tornadoes still be a reoccurring weather forecast we may never be able to predict? Will this ever end? Well, yeah because at some point your mental tornadoes must die – right? They obviously can't live forever. The way of the world is not a constant spinning tornado or a category 4/5 hurricane with wind gusts around 160 MPH. If only that prescription consisted of a pill that could relieve you of this madness. Unfortunately, the mental madness returns like the next hurricane season. At this point, you're ready to pull all your hair out and bang your head against the wall because you have a migraine from your thoughts. The agony of being alone is tormenting because who wants to be with someone who isolates themselves? Who wants to feel as though they're living the traumas because they're trying to be supportive? The patience one needs to be a supportive partner or spouse is immeasurable. However, it can be done. We as service members and veterans have a mission to seek as many resources as possible to aid in our mental awareness and recovery. In the event the recovery doesn't come as quickly as we'd like, there is still the possibility of gaining coping skills to better combat the tragedies that constantly set us off. You have a support system and I hope you utilize it because you deserve to be the best *YOU*, beyond all the trauma you've faced and may continue to face in the days, months, and years ahead.

RAPHAEL J. HOLMES, SSgt (Ret.)
United States Air Force
Operation Iraqi Freedom and Operation Enduring Freedom
(2006 – 2018)

Raphael J. Holmes is a Retired Air Force Veteran, musician, cook/caterer, and entrepreneur. He was born and raised in Jacksonville, North Carolina. He joined the Air Force in February 2006 and was fortunate to travel the world throughout his tenure in the military. While serving on active duty, he worked as a 2S, Material Management Specialist – also known as Logistics or Supply Chain Management. Raphael deployed to Kuwait, Qatar, and Afghanistan. All of which were during Operation Iraqi Freedom (OIF) and Operation Enduring Freedom (OEF).

After almost 13 years of active military service, Raphael was medically retired from the Air Force in October 2018 and transitioned to become an aspiring entrepreneur. Since his separation, he has completed a Bachelor of Arts degree in Project Management and is currently pursuing an MBA. Raphael enjoys quality time with family and friends; traveling; cooking; music, as well as playing the piano and organ; and laughing/joking.

Contact Information:
Raphael Holmes
Exotic Global Adventures (EGA) Travel Agency, Owner

For all traveling, catering, and music inquiries, contact via rjholmes8@gmail.com

PLAN AND PURPOSE

Kevin R. Richardson

I was born, May 1, 1960, in Holden, West Virginia; a small coal mining town about 60-miles southwest of the capital city of Charleston. It was there that I learned about the importance of family and later about God. In 1962, my father who worked for the local phone company was transferred to Washington, DC, where I spent the remainder of my life growing up. I graduated high school and proceeded onto college, but later left, got married, had a son and joined the U.S. Air Force. I would say that I had a plan, but God had a purpose for my life that still unfolds this very day.

Growing up in my family, particularly an African American family of the 50s and 60s, we had a deep sense of God. This was instilled by my late Grandfather, Deacon Lovell H. Richardson, Sr. He and my late grandmother had 11 children of their own and from their children there are about 80 grandchildren and at least 40 to 50 great-grandchildren. During our family reunions, we make it a point that we set time aside to honor God and our grandparents for their undying love for us.

As for me, I grew up a typical kid at the end of the civil rights movement, the War in Vietnam, and social awareness within our country. When our family arrived in Washington in 1962, we attended church almost regularly. But when we moved again in 1966, things started to change; we no longer attended church regularly, if at all. I began to feel that something was not quite right about all of this. Yet, when we would return to West Virginia, we would be in church with my extended family.

It wasn't until the death of the Reverend, Doctor Martin Luther King (1968), that something struck a chord with me. I later began to read every work that I could get my hands on about him, his life, and what he stood for. I studied him intently, which was my way of also understanding the will and purpose of God. I had begun to memorize many of his famous and not so famous speeches, that I was able to recite excerpts from memory.

It was Easter of 1971 that my life was about to be opened up in a more real way. My mother was invited to an Easter service with a co-worker, and she agreed to attend. My mother, sister, brother, and I attended that Sunday morning service, and I was so moved by all that had happened. I wanted to ask my mother about going back, but little did I realize, she had the same idea in mind. The very next Sunday, we returned and joined this church; we (my siblings and I) were later baptized and began our life in the church. For me, however, I felt that there was more, but I could not understand what it was at this time. As I grew older, I was involved in many of the youth activities of the church to later becoming a junior deacon, teacher, and working on the financial committee. But I still did not fully feel complete. When I reached high school, life opened up, teaching me the most prolific lessons that I would never forget.

This is the part where I'm supposed to say that I was a "straight A" student. On the contrary, I was an average student, just getting by. In high school, I majored in music (voice); this was a requirement to attend a school out of your zone. I also played in the marching band, jazz band and was even in the schools' gospel choir for a brief period. Music became a love, but I still had a problem. As an adolescent boy growing up, I discovered girls. adding to that problem was another problem; I loved to party. Partying seemed to be what I enjoyed the most. And it seemed that I enjoyed this even more than going to church. Sure, I had the church thing down, but I was missing that personal relationship with God. So, I was in church *playing church.*

One Thursday after school, during choir rehearsal a move of God came over some of the choir members; this we would normally say that they had gotten happy (in the Holy Ghost). This was an occurrence that I was very used to, but what happened next rocked me to my core. During this period, a member turned to the remainder of us and stated, that "if we did not do as they were doing, we were not saved." At this time, I witnessed a young lady in our group, who attended a Roman Catholic, burst into tears, and tore out of the room. I did not feel this was neither fair nor right for anyone to make this type of statement or pass this type of judgment. This had me reeling because I never knew that I had to be like others to prove my Christianity or salvation to anyone. That's when I left the choir at school, but I still sang in the ones at church.

This caused a spiral in my life where I experimented with marijuana and smoked cigarettes…not to mention the drinking. So, these were my vices along with trying to be the ladies' man. So, I did more parties, where I drank and smoked more, yet I was still going to church on Sunday mornings like nothing ever happened. While I was in this downward spiral, several significant events happened in my life which led to my ultimate decision to turn my life over to the Lord and to follow the will and purpose of God. When we were challenged in the choir rehearsal and with the young lady's abrupt departure, I began to ask the question; "with us reading the same book, The Holy Bible, why do we believe so differently?" So, I began to read the Bible, but I made one mistake. There was a saying that went around during that time, of which I cannot recall, and I shouted it to the other group of students one day during lunch. I was then questioned as to where did I get this saying? My reply, naturally, was in the Bible. Well, I learned a valuable lesson that if you say it is in the Bible, you'd better be ready to produce chapter and verse. Neither of which I was able to do.

I went home that night quite despondent from my very embarrassing moment at school. I tore open the Bible and began to read it. I could not get past the book of Genesis. Being frustrated, I went to the end of the book and began to read from Revelation backwards. I did this in about two or three days completing in the book of Genesis.

It was Christmas Eve, Thursday, December 24, 1979; I was on my way to home of my then girlfriend. I was excited about giving her, her gift of a ring. As I began to travel to her home, it began to rain very heavily. As I was traveling along on the rain-soaked highway, out of nowhere a red car shot past me causing me to lose control of my car. As my car was careening out of control, it seemed to be heading to a ditch. In that ditch, I witnessed death himself awaiting me. I began to pray; "Lord, if I am to crash and even die, let no one else lose their life on my account. And whatever it is that I'm to do, I am more than willing to follow through.

It seemed that at the moment I ended that prayer, the car came to a complete stop across three lanes of traffic. Thankfully, no cars were near me for about a mile or so, giving ample time to gingerly move my car over to the shoulder of the road and gain my composure. Sometime later, I was alone and prayed, asking God "what it is that I'm to do?"

One night I had my Bible on the table, wondering where and what I should read to find direction, but I did not understand the Bible thoroughly. Again, I prayed and asked God "what it is that He was conveying to me?" I said, "when I open this book, let the pages fall to what is to be revealed to me." I grabbed the cover with both hands and let them fall open on the table. It fell to Isaiah 61, where it reads: *"The Spirit of the Lord God is upon me; because the Lord has anointed me to preach good tidings unto the meek; he hath sent me to bind up the brokenhearted, to proclaim liberty to the captives and the opening of the prison to them that are bound; To proclaim the acceptable year of the Lord..."* For fear, I immediately closed the Bible feeling that God made a grave mistake yet, I asked two additional times and each time the Bible fell to this very same scripture. I immediately fell on my knees asking God for His divine guidance and to make me into a vessel that would be pleasing to Him.

In January of 1980, I made my public declaration before the church congregation of God's call on my life and my pastor began to work with me, training me in ministry. I later joined the U.S. Air Force after losing a federal job in Washington. Through this adventure, I landed at Carswell AFB and God allowed me to join a church in the city of Fort Worth, Texas, where I continued working with the pastor there. It was there where I was licensed into the Gospel Ministry.

By this time, I thought life would be easy for me, being in a new setting and lifestyle, but it became more challenging than ever. Upon arriving at my first assignment as a "Bomb-Loader" on B-52 aircraft, my first supervisor made it up in his mind that I was not the type of person the Air Force needed. So, he intentionally used my race against me, which the whole Weapons Shop could see, but no one said a word. For one year, the contention was so thick, you could cut it with a knife. Because of this, I was forced to learn my job by way of regulations, technical data (Tech Data) and other such resources that would ensure that I did what I was assigned to the letter.

Well, this didn't sit well with my immediate supervisor. One day, while working on a piece of "Off Equipment," which is equipment that is removed from an aircraft for maintenance and servicing, I had everything the Tech Data specified for me to have to do my work. He came along and without warning, shoved everything from the workbench onto the floor. I had had it up to that point. I immediately asked him, "what does he have against me," to which he replied, "I got nothing against you; boy!!!!" Right there I had enough, to which I suggested that we go "old school" behind the woodshed. Yes, I challenged him and hoped that he'd wind, because I was going to try my best to hurt him. He later retorted; "do you know what you're doing???" I replied, "yes, and if you write the Article 15, I'm going to kill you."

I was later called into the office by my shop chief, after which I was reassigned to another supervisor. With this change in management, I learned everything about a B-52 aircraft under this new supervisor and I started to like serving. However, the church was not what I thought it was, as I was looking for what I was used to back in my hometown. So, I submitted to swap with another Airman, serving at Langley AFB, Virginia. He didn't like the east coast, and I thought this would be a bonus for me, serving and living near my hometown. So, upon our commander's approval, I was heading to now be a bomb-loader on F-15 aircraft. Upon my arrival there, the assignment seemed to be what I wanted and as a bonus, I took up driving tour buses part-time.

It was at Langley, I left the perfect will of God, for His permissive will. During my 18-months there, I was moving further and further away from the God, I professed earlier. I didn't attend church, nor stayed in the Word of God for direction. Military Temporary Duty (TDY) and Motorcoach travels consumed my every moment so much so that I had forsaken God, my family and even myself. It got so that I didn't care even if I stayed married anymore. I just wanted to enjoy life, so I thought in this way. Sadly, my little 3-and-a-half-year career in the Air Force was waning too. After much frustration, I decided to put in for a new occupation, to which I was accepted to retrain to become a Training Specialist. After receiving my acceptance to retrain, I immediately received my assignment orders to return to Fort Worth, Texas.

So, off to Technical (Tech) School I departed, leaving all behind me including leaving my family. I thought it would be a good time to restart my life... But wouldn't you know it, I once heard *"the best laid plans can go awry..."* and they did. After returning to Carswell, the first base where I served, I got to meet up with some of my old friends still assigned and to make it a point to make new ones. However, God has a way of dealing with you even when you're not keeping Him on your mind. While I thought I would redo my life over again in Fort Worth, God made it possible for me and my family to come back together again. This time, life was even better than before. We returned to the church I departed and within one month of ordination, I was transferred to the United Kingdom (UK), where I later served as pastor of a church and served as president of a fellowship of 22 American-led churches throughout the UK.

Upon my return to the States, I was the Wing Training Manager for the DC Air National Guard. I also served as the Executive Assistant to the pastor of the church I formerly attended. I served with the Chaplains ministry of the DC Air National Guard and the National Guard Bureau, where I formerly served. I also served with other clergy persons as we assisted the DC Metropolitan Police Department with their task of notifying family members of their loved ones who were victims of homicide. Now, I currently serve as Pastor of a local church, and was consecrated a Bishop in the Lord's Church. I'm grateful for a wife and children who stood by me because I know it was not easy for them, yet God brought us through. For this, I give Him praise.

Again, I had a plan, but God had a purpose and with this, I have learned what Proverbs 3:5-6 says to: *"Trust in the Lord with all of your heart, not leaning to your own understanding. In all your ways acknowledge Him and He will direct your paths."* He has allowed me to complete 29 years of Military service and 40 years of ministry. Sounds like a perfect plan on purpose to me.

KEVIN R. RICHARDSON, SMSgt (Ret.)
United States Air Force
(1982 – 2011)

Kevin R. Richardson served 29 years in the United States Air Force, as an Aircraft Weapons Loader, Unit/Wing Training Manager, Support Liaison of the Chapel Ministry with the District of Columbia (DC) Air National Guard and Chief of Protocol to the Director of the Air National Guard at the National Guard Bureau, Washington, DC

Kevin R. Richardson serves as the pastor of Hope Fellowship Church in Suitland, Maryland and was consecrated a Bishop in the Lord's Church in August 2019. He served as a member of the faculty with the Southern Baptist Church Bible College in Washington, DC and as the Executive Assistant and Chief Adjutant to Bishop Robert

E. White, pastor of the New Hope Baptist Church in Forestville, Maryland. He rendered service as a representative of the Clergy Response Team for the Washington (DC) Metropolitan Police Department.

He answered the call to the gospel ministry (1980). During his service with the United States Air Force, he was license to preach (1982) and ordained (1988) and pastored the Gospel Service of Royal Air Force (RAF) Bentwaters, in the United Kingdom (UK) from 1989-1992. During this time, he also presided over the United Kingdom Christian Fellowship (UKCF); a fellowship representing 26 American led churches throughout the UK.

SMSgt Richardson has completed an Associate of Applied Science Degree in Educational & Instructional Technology from the Community College of the Air Force, a Bachelor of Arts Degree in Religious Studies, and a Master of Arts Degree in Practical Theology, both from Regent University. He is married to the former Minister Celeste D. Burgess and has three adult children: Kevin II, Janee and Karlette; a granddaughter (Avery Monet) and two grandsons (Josiah Maxwell and Desmond Taylor).

RESILIENCE UNDER FIRE

Tangella R. Brown

I'm a 28-year retired Air Force Chief. Chief. Yes, that sounds good and amazing, and really, it is. But like any other position of authority, it doesn't come without its challenges.

I was born and raised in a small town in Arkansas and graduated with honors. I was my Senior Class President, and we wanted the legacy of the class of 1988 to be that our graduating class would be the first class in the history of our high school to have an integrated prom. Yes, that's what I said, the first integrated prom in the history of Forrest City High School, a school that had been integrated for 25 years, just now having a prom where the white kids and the black kids could celebrate together. So, as you can imagine, this was no place to expand ones' thinking. So, what happens when a student in the top 10% of their graduating class decides that they need to go to college, but "just not now?" For me, the answer was easy, I would join the military, I would get my college degree and I would get out in four years. Well, four career changes, 28 years, five months and 19 days later, I finally got out.

When I joined, I didn't know what I really wanted to do so I took the ASVAB and went into the Air Force "Open Admin," meaning that whatever job the Air Force wanted me to have, is the job I would have. For me that job was Morse Code. Morse Code! Okay, so I'm dating myself. While in basic training, I took a test where I was taught Dits and Dahs and within a few minutes I had to remember them and copy them as I heard them. While I was taking the test, I just knew that I was going to get stuck in a job that I didn't want. But as much as I wanted to fail the test, there was something in me that wouldn't let me fail, so, I passed the test and I was off to Ft. Devens in Massachusetts for technical training for what could be anywhere from six months to a year and then, if selected, on to Cory Station in Florida for advanced training. For me, advance training was something I wanted to do right off the bat, but "Uncle Sam" decided that someone else would go…that is, until my last week in training when the person they had selected failed out of training and couldn't go. I was now the new "best choice." I had to learn quickly that this way of doing things was going to be my new norm. Things were not going to happen when or how I thought they would, but that God was in control of my steps.

My first duty assignment as a code-copying Airman was required to be overseas, so I volunteered for an English-speaking country…I thought I'd keep it simple. I was stationed at Chicksands AB, UK and two years later I retrained into Information Management. By this time, I was right around four years in the Air Force, and I did not have my degree as I promised myself I would, so getting out of the military at the four-year mark was no longer an option. Shortly after that I was back on Chicksands AB copying Morse Code again for one more year, until the base closed, at which time I retrained again as a Personnel Specialist. Now, to have this job as a Morse Code operator, I had to get and maintain a Top-Secret Security Clearance. That was easy. I was a small-town girl, raised in a Christian family and wasn't allowed to do much to get into trouble (thanks mom and dad). So, when I got my security clearance, someone told me, "Once you get your clearance, always keep a job that requires a clearance." Still very much green, I didn't understand the importance of that, but I kept that advice close to my heart. One day, while at Pope AFB, North Carolina some Flight Attendants came through and stopped by and mentioned the idea of being a Flight Attendant. I didn't know the Air Force had such a thing, but I wasn't interested because I had no desire to go to Washington, DC…I still had the small-town mentality and wasn't ready to make the transition, but I kept that close to my heart as well.

My last Personnel Specialist job was at Ft Bragg, North Carolina on the Special Operations compound and I didn't know what my options for jobs with a security clearance would be once I left there. But when time came to leave, the stars began to line up. I started looking for "Special Duty" jobs that required a Security Clearance, and what do you know, Flight Attendant came up, but the job would require me to live in the Washington, DC metro. I had to ask myself 'what was more important, keeping my security clearance or facing my "big city" fears,' so I applied and was accepted, and I was on my way to DC.

Little did I know, soon after taking this "Special Duty" job, it would turn into a bonified Air Force Specialty, and I was going to have to make a decision. Would I go back to my AFSC as a Personnel Specialist, or would I keep this job as a Flight Attendant and keep my security clearance? Side bar: One day someone told me "If you stay in this job (Flight Attendant) long enough, you'll eventually make Chief." Not knowing if there was a real chance that I could make Chief, I kept that close to heart as well.

Fast-forward 10 years, having seen the politics that go along with being a Senior NCO, I really didn't have the desire to be an Air Force Chief. I figured, I'd finally gotten my college degree…ok so, I'm an over-achiever, I got six degrees, including my Master's Degree…I figured 20 years and E-7 was enough for me…time for me to move along and start another career…or so I thought. At the 19-year mark, I was selected for promotion to Senior Master Sergeant. Everybody wanted to know "how did you do it, what did you do to get promoted?" One would think "it was about time…19 years." My answer was that "The Lord GAVE it to me." You see, I knew that I had done NOTHING worthy of promotion. After all, I was a terrible test taker, but I also knew that if my supervisors and leaders said go to school, I went to school; if they said, participate in this or that, that's what I did. I did what was required of me instead of questioning or complaining about the process. After all, they had been around much longer than I had. Later on, I found out that no one in my career field had ever been promoted to Senior Master Sergeant their first-time testing, and that's when I really knew, that the Lord had given me this promotion. At this point I thought "ok Lord, I guess you know better than I do what's best for my life...after all, you have been guiding my foot-steps since I enlisted." So, I took the promotion. And this is where it began to get really real.

Although I realized that there was a bit of politics that went along with being in the Top-3, up until now, I thought somehow that I would be immune to it all...after all, I don't do politics. Boy was I wrong. My other Senior and Chief Master Sergeant friends began telling me how bad things were in their leadership position and tried very hard to prepare me for what was to come, because they knew that one day, I'd be taking their place. Things were sometimes so bad for them, that from time to time the six of us (all black females, E-7 to E-9) would meet in one person's office and pray that the Lord would come in and move. Now, I still wasn't privy to everything that was happening, and I thought, surely, it can't be that bad, but still we prayed.

And then it happened, the first day that I began to lead my career field as the 3rd of what would be four consecutive black female Chiefs (five, if you count the one black female who was recruited from active duty as a SMSgt to lead the Airmen in the ANG with a promotion to Chief Master Sergeant) in our career field, reality began to set in. From day one, the finger-pointing began about problems that existed before I arrived. No problem, I thought, I'm the Chief now, let's fix it. I wasn't going to pass the buck or point the finger. I was the face of the career field now! But I didn't know that nothing I would do or say was every going to be enough. How could I have ever imagined that my fellow Chiefs would dismiss my decisions; the Wing Commander would put me in front of a group of peers and Commanders for the sole purpose of trying to embarrass and discredit me; or that other Chiefs from the Command who had never met me were going to do all they could to discredit me as a person. Certainly, I couldn't have guessed that my own Group Commander would refuse to support me, regardless of the evidence that my decisions were sound; not to mention that whenever something didn't go as planned, I was going to go out of my way to make it right. The final straw came when I was replaced by another Chief while I was still in the position.

You see, the issue was that I wasn't going to allow people outside the career field to make decisions about a career field they had never worked in without sufficient dialogue and ideas that made sense. I couldn't just roll over and 'say yes' to ideas that were not in the best interest of my airmen…airmen who worked their butts off every day to ensure the comfort, safety and security of our customers. I was, however, open to conversation that made sense and supported the airmen I was in charge of. I had to learn quickly that doing what's right concerning the people you represent wasn't always as important to some people as making a name for themselves and making changes just to be able to say they made a change. Don't get me wrong – I'm not anti-change, there just has to be a need and it has to make sense. For that line of thinking, I was going to be broken and discredited at all costs. It didn't matter that I was looking out for the best interest of my airmen in a leadership position, while still flying the line whenever called upon. I was going to be made an example of and made to fall in line with the majority.

It came to the point that I didn't know who to trust, but I was NOT going to fail my airmen. Every morning, I would literally roll out of bed and onto the floor and pray "Lord, if you don't go in before me today, I won't make it." I would cry and sometimes I wouldn't even want to get out of bed, but I couldn't let them take my sanity. I couldn't let them take my joy and I couldn't give up on my airmen. And then one day the Lord said, "I gave you Chief. I didn't promise you 30 (years)" so I knew it was time for me to gracefully bow out. By this time, I wanted 30 years, after all, the other Chiefs who had paved the way for me had done 30, and I wanted it, too. But that was not God's plan me. I had to realize that He had already done something even greater. He had given me something, that, unless I actually did something wrong or illegal, none of them could take away from me…Chief!

The Lord had done more for me than I ever could have imagined. He ordered every single assignment and every single promotion, but He didn't promise me that every day would be sunny; however, He did know how to keep me on my knees. And here's the kicker… When I retired, I got phone calls with statements like "the people who didn't have anything nice to say about you, can't stop singing your praises" and "they don't know how you got it done; how you always made your quota, and your replacement can't seem to get it done like you did." "How did you do it?" I did it by the help of the Lord. I always listened to those who had gone before me, even when I didn't know what it meant, but most of all, my entire life and career had always been guided by the Lord.

If there's anything I learned in my 28 years of service, it's that the military is an extension of life; it's a job like any other job, and like any other occupation or organization that you join, you must be willing to abide by the rules and regulations of that place in order to succeed. I learned to appreciate the guidance of those who had paved the way for me to follow, and that when someone gave me a tool (advice) I'd never used before, not to just throw it away, instead, learn how to use it because although I may not have needed it that day, there was going to come a time that I would need that tool, and in the heat of the battle was not the time to try and learn how to use it. As a Believer, I realized that God didn't allow anything to happen to me that He couldn't use in my life as a testimony. But, most of all, I learned that if God truly was the head of my life, I had to be willing to endure the rain that came into my life, because along with the sun, it made for a great harvest. It's been almost 35 years and I still have that security clearance today.

TANGELLA R. BROWN, CMSgt (Ret.)
United States Air Force
Operation Iraqi Freedom
(1988 – 2017)

Tangella Brown is a 28-year retired Air Force Chief Master Sergeant. She completed her Air Force career with four career specialties, including Morse Code, Information Management, Personnel Management, and she retired as the Career Advisor for all Air Force Flight Attendants. Tangella flew as the lead Flight Attendant for the Vice President of the United States, the First Lady, members of Congress and cabinet members for 17 years where she was able to travel extensively around the world. She currently resides in the North Texas Metro where she is a Minister and the Minister of Music at the Church of the Living God, Plano, Texas.

Tangella is the host of a Podcast "Traveling Through the Word with T," where she delivers her take on Bible stories, and she is an Audio/Visual specialist, producing live streams and editing video for churches on the East Coast. She studied at Webster University where she graduated with a Master's Degree in Procurement & Contracting. When not editing videos, she can usually be found sitting behind her desk searching the web for the latest and greatest Tech projects like the Magic Mirror and building them for just fun.

Tangella R. Brown, Minister
Phone: (301) 442-6042
Email: tavicreations1@gmail.com
Website: www.TAVICreations.com

TEARS BEHIND A FITTED MASK

LaTorcha R. Polati

As I lean against the shower walls allowing the water to wash away the tears that run down my face, I was in a battle for my life, for my mind, for my marriage, and for my sanity. An unseen battle that I could not use these hands and punch someone in the face. I couldn't push hard enough naturally to knock this enemy down as it constantly played peek-a-boo with my already shattered emotions trying to show that all I have been through that he was still able to sneak in stealth mode.

The thoughts of inadequacy, worthlessness, fear, disappointments, and confusion hit me all at once. The noise from the enemy started as a whisper but turned to screams. Why? Because in my weakness, I acknowledged that I could hear what the enemy said. I was that woman again, the one that securely placed the mask on the brokenness hiding the tears that fell behind the mask.

I didn't realize the lie, betrayal, termination, and the transition were so traumatic until I walked back on the base in Italy. The anxiety gripped my heart as if it was a vice-grip securely fastened around the head of the screw, the mind-fog encamped my head as if it was determined to distort the already cloudy vision of what I could see. As I tried to catch my breath, which felt like hot steaming lava pouring in and out of my lungs so strongly, I was sure that a fainting spell would find me as I walked down the street where I was once escorted. The overwhelming urge to run away consumed every fiber of my being. The tears slowly flowed, which I knew because of the saltiness, as the flash back of my ordeals rewound like an old cassette player I played in the late '80s. Here I was again in a place I swore I would never go back to, yet I was thrust back to relive the ordeals over again.

As Italy is a beautiful place with amazing food and breath-taking scenery, it was also one of the most traumatic assignments that I had…going from being a single mom to married; from being a soldier to a civilian; then from being employed to fired. My marriage was not as solid as I hoped at that time because I felt that being married made me make choices that I probably would not have made. But I just tugged the strings of my tightly fitted mask, squared my shoulders and made it happen…day after day crumbling from the weight of the invisible mask that I learned to apply many years ago.

A mask that had me feeling like a fraud wondering if the mask would slip and the people would see that I was not as strong and resilient as I portrayed to be. Instead, I walked in low self-esteem and self-hatred not in the confidence that demanded attention and respect even though that was what I received. I was the one sought after for financial matters that needed to be solved, housing issues that needed to be fixed, life issues that needed to be corrected, yet I was running away from myself daily.

My mask was applied when my commander (many years before Italy) pinned me against the wall in my apartment I shared with my daughter (who was not there at the time). In his eyes, I could see that he had checked out and evil replaced the man I trusted with my life. It wasn't until he was finished that he changed back becoming apologetic as he cleaned the remains of his DNA from the walls of my apartment. The tears fell every day since that day behind the tightly fitted mask that showed the world that I was present even when I was not. I was a Christian woman who loved God yet walked in shame.

The untraceable tears fell as a member of command team called my C.O.C. (Chain of Command) because he noticed the infatuation that the Commander, Sergeant Major, and First Sergeant all had of me. They wanted *a touch* for whatever the reason and was determined to have it by any means necessary even if it was to brush too close to me in passing. A fake meeting to call me in the office behind closed doors to ask *if we could do "that" again* as the evil jumped in and out of his eyes. Stevie Wonder sung a soulful song about the tears of a clown that fell when no one was around.

Well, Mr. Wonder let me tell you about the tears that fell behind the mask when everyone was around. I had to learn to control my voice so that it would not crack...control my posture so no one would see me slouch…control my walk so my knees would not buckle under the weight of what I carried…control the pitch of my laughter so it could drown out the internal whimper and outburst of cries filled with uncontrollable tears.

I was determined to become a leader so I would not have to deal with issues like that. As my rank grew, so did the weight of the mask. I was looked at differently than my male counter parts when I ran circles around them. I took from my family to ensure that I was everything that the Army needed, but just like that commander I was betrayed by the Army.

The weight of the mask, years of untraceable tears, and silent cries presented itself physically in my body as I served in Italy. I had reoccurring cysts that doubled me over in pain…that took my unborn child allowing him/her not to grow…that caused me to have many surgeries. I was at a point that the pain would not leave although there was no physical reason that it should be there because the ovary was not there; yet my silent cries still remained fueling the pain.

I was assigned to the Wounded Warrior Battalion (WWB) away from my soldiers and my unit and was notified that if I didn't get better, I would be medically retired from the United States Army after serving my country for over 20 years. While in WWB, I started an internship with one of the offices on base, which led me to receiving a permanent position as a GS-11. I thought I had found my dream job, which I loved because it allowed me to still assist the soldiers, civilians, and contractors assigned to Italy. Just as in the military, I was the one that everyone came to in order to get things fixed, corrected, and processed. I worked two positions, one above my pay grade (GS-12), while doing the work I was hired to do. For about six months or so everything was great until the new arrival to the organization.

Almost immediately upon of his arrival, his aggressiveness in action and speech triggered me into reliving my trauma that I had experienced by the hands of my commander years. I had not removed the mask, but I really believed that as a civilian, I could slowly learn to loosen the ties. Again, my tears fell behind my once again well fitted mask. But this was worse because I was on probation as a government service employee, which meant I had to play by their rules as it was an unspoken role that you could be fired for any reason until you became permanent.

The more I put my head down and focused on my job the more he harassed me while creating a hostile environment. He was determined to make my life a living hell. He slowly turned many of my co-workers against me by talking negatively towards me, belittling me every chance he got, and he criticized the work I did for the organization.

I found myself in the bathroom crying into my hands as I could feel the pressure of being pushed against the wall over and over again. I hated my situation because I felt trapped as if I had no choice but to deal with this if I wanted to remain in Italy with my husband. I couldn't talk to my husband because he was not aware of what happened with my commander, yet I blamed him. I was going into counseling sessions with my therapist to talk about the man who now made me feel assaulted every daily.

I had learned how to look like I was breathing normally while I was hyperventilating. All they could see was the invisible mask that smiled and knew how and when to nod. Even though I was dying daily, I never allowed my distress to show because I had tightly fitted the mask I had worn; I had to present perfection in all that I did. I had been trained to put my best foot forward, never let them see you sweat, while you suck it up buttercup.

The strong exterior I constructed like a fortified dam presented a crack where the leak formed unseen pressure threatening the very dam itself with a possible explosion. You see, not only did I have on the mask, but I also felt as if I was assaulted every day while the hands of the GS probation system cupped my mouth closed.

At my breaking point, I reached out for a life preserver. I sent an email to my immediate supervisor with the subject line, "Hostile Environment," as my external cry for help. Within the body of the email I stated, *"I am in a hostile environment, and it is starting to affect me (panic attacks, anxiety). I do not want to interact with him because it is always a struggle to get simple things done.* Later in the in the email I stated, "*I feel like I am in Afghanistan constantly on guard.*"

I closed the email with, "*I am **begging** you to help me because I don't know how much more of this I can take.*" Unbeknownst to him, some familiar spirits found themselves lingering around me again – the spirits of suicide and depression. Anything had to be better than feeling like this. Because of the head fog, I could not think of the right thing to do. My cries fell to the ground.

Now I cried untraceable tears behind a fitted mask. I felt assaulted every day, the hands of the GS probation system cupped my mouth closed, and I toyed with suicide and depression. Now a new set of hands belonging to my supervisor appeared seeking to mute my already muffled cry.

Days went by, and I forwarded the email again to the supervisor as I blind copied it to his supervisor in an attempt to get help. I cried louder now feeling vulnerable because they all knew but didn't do anything. The aggressiveness got worse as the hands from my supervisor's supervisor was placed over my mouth, because we had to present that we had the best organization, and everything was perfect.

I was in a room full of men with their hands securely clamped down over my mouth drowning out my cries for help yet calling it a meeting. I wanted to discuss all of the issues, but I became triggered, frightened, and basically shut down because I felt like a rape victim facing the rapist in a court room detailing the events of my assault.

The man that I created the complaint about now came after me with a vengeance. Without authorization, he reviewed my PII (personally identifiable information) and sought to find something to remove me. As we all know that is retaliation. That's when it happened. The hands of my assailant gripped the hands of the others around my mouth to silence my muffled cries.

I had nowhere to turn, no one to talk to so I cried out to God because this was life or death. I am not sure if I wore the mask before God, but I asked Him to expose them for what they were doing to me. Trusting that God would expose them, I waited, and I got fired. I was humiliated, belittled, and treated unfairly.

You may be asking yourself, "I thought she asked God to expose them, but she got fired?" You see, God did just what I asked Him to do – expose. He exposed me to me, which took me to a low place where I had no other option but to look up and give Him a true YES. A 'yes' that changed the trajectory of my life. God exposed the lies that I had believed for many years, so He helped me to remove my well-fitted mask, rewrite my story dictated by Him, and become the woman of purpose that I was meant to be. I became a Minister of the Gospel, a certified Christian Life Coach so I can help and hear the silent cries of the woman behind the mask. I became the CEO and Founder of Determined Steps, LLC. To become anything that you want to be, you must first take determined steps to achieve it. *"A man's heart plans his way, but the LORD determines his steps"* (Proverbs 16:9).

LATORCHA RENA POLATI, SFC (Ret.)
United States Army
*Operation Restore Hope, Operation Uphold Democracy,
Operation Enduring Freedom*
(1992 – 2016)

LaTorcha Rena Polati is a native of Danville, Virginia. LaTorcha Rena Polati is a disabled veteran, a survivor of sexual trauma, wife, mother, Minister, certified Christian Life Coach, consultant, mentor, speaker, and mindset Strategist.

She is also the founder and CEO of Determined Steps, LLC, a Christian Life Coaching business. Determined Steps, LLC was developed to move women from brokenness to walking in newness of life, by bridging the gap between mental and spiritual healing. She has been anointed to assist women in removing the invisible mask, rewriting their story the way God dictated and living life authentically. She empowers women to move forward one Determined Step at a time. She has the ability to hear women's silent cries and cultivate space for them to be seen, heard, and healed while ushering in breakthrough to freedom in Christ.

LaTorcha believes every woman has the ability to live life unapologetically when surrounded by a strong circle of support coupled with guidance to implement sustainable life changes.

LaTorcha's ministry and business can be experienced through her website, YouTube, and Facebook. She is the Host of a weekly virtual show via Facebook Live called Bridging the Gap which can be viewed at:

Website
www.latorchapolati.com

Facebook personal
https://www.facebook.com/highly.favored.733

Facebook business
https://www.facebook.com/determinedsteps

Facebook group (Women Chosen by God, Aligned by Purpose)
https://www.facebook.com/groups/2527539924207121

Linkedin
https://www.linkedin.com/in/latorcha-polati-90737134

Instagram
@I_am_LaTorcha_Polati

THE DAY I RETIRED, LIFE BEGAN

Sonya Mills-McCall

On Dec 1, 2008, I received my USAF military Certificate of Retirement! I had successfully completed 26 plus years (1982-2008) of service to God and country under several presidents. I was only 48 years young and retiring from a job that would pay me for the rest of my life. I could not wait to move south (Florida) and start life with my then 12-year young daughter. I had four children at the time, ages 33, 30, 29, and 14. I envisioned being able to be at every school event, the involved parent known at the school. See, my travels in the military did not allow me to be that as much as I wanted. There's so much I could share but let me condense it into segments of Trial and Tribulations to Triumph!

Trials & Tribulations...

In 1982, I along with two other friends, traveled to Dannelly Air National Guard Base and decided to meet a recruiter to take the ASVAB and become members of the 187th Reconnaissance Wing on the buddy plan. One of my friends aced the test but was disqualified for medical reasons. I and the other moved forward and raised our right hand to a six-year commitment to the United States Air Force. Once it was determined what our job / Air Force Specialty Code (AFSC) would be, dates were given for us to go to basic training and on to technical school. No one shared that since our schools were starting at two separate times, we would no longer be able to go in on the buddy plan. Scared, my confidence fading, I wanted to back out because I did not want to go alone.

Well, my smart friend said; "Sis, we need to do this for our children." Oh, did I mention we were both single parents at the time. Off to basic training we go, a few weeks apart, never seeing the other one while assigned to Lackland Air Force Base, San Antonio, Texas. We now travel to our schools which were held at Keesler Air Force Base, Biloxi, Mississippi. By the time my friend got to her school, I was graduating and heading back to Montgomery, AL. It was this trial of entering the military that assisted me in growing my personal characteristics of integrity, compassion, and persistence, along with leadership, communication, and analytical skills.

Disappointed that I was now on this journey alone, I was unsure if I would stay. Mentally I was going to do my 6-year commitment and call it a day! You know in the world of law when one goes to trial there is a jury and a judge. My jury was my military assignment, while my judge was God. You may ask how is that possible, Sonya. See, as I awoke each day and before going to bed each night, my prayer life increased with one consistent request of my judge: "God, please get me through this six-year commitment." There were days it was a struggle. It's 1988 and I must reenlist or end this military journey. Enjoying my guard unit and summer camps, I reenlist!

Let's fast forward to December 1989. I am glad my judge and jury during my trials were God the Father, Son, and Holy Ghost! I applied for and was hired to go active duty at the Air National Guard Bureau as a Command Post Controller. My report date was January 15, 1990, where I signed in at the 201st Mission Support Squadron. There I met the most pleasant and helpful airman. If this is what active duty is all about, I am going to enjoy this two-year tour of duty. Those two years turned into 18 years and 10 months of emotions from happiness to sadness and a host of other reactions.

Well, my job would be in the Command Post, the eyes and ears for the General. It started out to be a pleasant environment until the day I received the call that my mom was in the hospital and needed surgery for stage-3 colon cancer. Having been on the job less than two months, I was told I had 2.5 days of leave, and could go home for two days. Nope – I did not read the fine print on the contract of becoming an active-duty airman. I was like, *excuse me?* What I was aware of was that there was someone in charge of the person denying my leave. So, I went to the next person, was granted the leave, and told them I would keep them posted on my mom status. I quickly gathered my things, stopped by base operations and there was a plane leaving that afternoon for Maxwell AFB. I knew then God had me.

I make it home; mom has surgery and my siblings, and I are told she would still need chemo and 28 radiation treatments. I called back to ask for an extension on my leave. Faced with opposition, I know God was looking out for me because I shared with the supervisor, "Sir I will be seeing about my mom, and I will take whatever consequences when or if I return." I was home about 10 additional days. Now it's going to take me 4-months to pay back the leave I have used. I won't be able to see my mom for a while. Guess what? We worked 12-hour shifts, three days on and three days off and most every time I had my 3-days off there was a plane coming to Maxwell AFB if only for a day or two, yet long enough for me to spend a couple hours with my mom.

Let's fast forward several years...I get a call that my mom has been in a car accident and is hospitalized in Mississippi. She has several broken ribs and a broken pelvis. I notify my supervisor, the young man that was against my going home in 1990. Hmmm...now *you* can take off because your dog is having puppies and I can't take off to see about my mom? The devil is a liar! The woman who has always been my protector and provider, she stuck with me and ensured that I kept focused even after becoming a teenage mother. It was the guidance of my mother that made sure I still graduated with my class. She gave me the responsibility of caring for my baby but would make sure I had time to study and keep my grades up – so there was NO way I was not going to be there for her during this time. Once again, God (my Judge) made a way. Yes, again I had to go to the commander who not only approved my staying as long as it took to take care of the affairs, but when I returned, I was to make an appointment to meet with him. I am shouting as I write this because I know under other circumstances, I would have been reprimanded and given an article 15 for being insubordinate – but God (my Judge)! Not only did none of that happen but upon my return and meeting with the commander he moved me from the Command Post to the Chief of Chaplains Office to work on the Family Enrichment Team.

About a month after being assigned to the Chaplains Office, my husband was diagnosed with a rare form of cancer and the doctors said he had about three months to live. This journey was much easier working in the chaplain's office. I was given all the time needed to make the next three months with my family the best it could be. God had other plans. Three months came, four months came, a year came, and we are still enjoying life together. My trial is now turning into a triumph! Doctors at Walter Reed were in awe and admitted they were not sure how my husband was still alive, but whatever he was doing he should continue to do because it was nothing they were doing. My husband did not make his transition until January 1, 2007. You do the math! My Judge turned three months into eight years. Thank you, God, for TRIUMPH!

My TRIUMPH...

Continuing to December 1, 2008 – my official date of retirement – the trials I had to endure were now becoming my triumph. Retired at the age of 48! My Judge (God) kept blessing me because in six months from retirement (May 2009), I received the letter many said would take years; the letter was from the Florida Veterans Affairs awarding me 100% veteran disability. You're saying what's so special about that, Sonya? Who wants to be disabled? Having been married for twenty plus years to a Vietnam veteran, I watched him fight, struggle, and die awaiting a VA disability rating. Though he did not receive his disability, I did.

Our daughter can attend any Alabama public college for "FREE" since I entered military service in the state of Alabama. She graduated with a bachelor's in criminal justice from Alabama State University. The triumph does not stop there. I was blessed to return to Alabama to care for my then 80-year young mother, who was full of life and joy, the epitome of unconditional love. She taught me how to be a servant in the house of the Lord, as well as how to serve those chosen by God to lead His people. My triumph came from giving back to her what she had given to me, my siblings, and my friends. She had many sons and daughters because her house was always opened to others. She fed the community. She would always say, "I may not have much, but I can always feed you." She loved caring for the babies.

While visiting Georgia in 2015, she had a stroke, and her health began to deteriorate. You are wandering how is this a triumph? This journey with my mom taught me how to meet people where they are…To love on them even when they are unsure of how to love you back. She became my baby and I cared for her as if she was an infant. She developed stroke-induced Dementia which changed our lives medically and physically but not mentally. Having to care for her 24/7, I would not change any of it. When she felt her time was nearing, she knew I wanted to live in Montgomery and agreed that if I found a home in Montgomery, she would move with me from Selma.

We moved in May 2016 and the next five months had highs and lows. My mom, an original "Foot Soldier" in the Selma to Montgomery Civil Rights movement, loved Selma. For her to agree to move back to Montgomery meant the world to me cause even in her aging years she would still do what she felt made her children happy. With assistance from my siblings, children, nieces, nephews, and good friends, we traveled this journey until October 23, 2016. Her transition was a triumph because I believe she had spoken with her Lord and Savior and was ready to take her resting place until the rapture. Even though she was struggling with that terrible disease, she wanted to make sure I was okay before she transitioned. She would constantly share with me that God will take care of her, and He loved me enough to take of me as well.

Trials were the epitome and foundation I needed to build life after retirement. Veterans often see obstacles and struggles as barriers to figuring out what to do next. Mine made me more resilient and my heart to serve increased. My trials empowered me to study God's word, which encouraged me as I meditated and prayed. I would exercise, do deep breathing exercises, but most of all I developed an attitude of gratitude. Before getting up and/or going to bed, I thanked God for ALL things that would be before me; the good, bad, and ugly. God allowed me to jump in deep water, yet He never allowed me to drown. He was equipping me with skills of servitude, empathy, agape love, and more to serve my fellow airman, family, and strangers. I put my ego on the shelf and began sharing my trials, tribulations, and testimony by using my Critical Incident Stress Management (CISM) and Applied Suicide Intervention Skills Training (ASIST). My mindset switched from being angry and hurt, to being humble and grateful that God trusted me with trials to be an overcomer. Always a servant, I want to do more. Some say, "You do too much;" but I say, "I don't do enough."

When I say that through my trials, God has been my Judge – He was in control, and I give Him all the glory and praise. Thirteen years since retirement and my life is still full of TRIUMPH! I praise Him every day. I'm reminded of Jeremiah 29:11 which says, *"For I know the plans I have for you, declares the Lord, plans to prosper you, and not to harm you, plans to give you hope and a future."* I am living my future! Remember: When God is your Judge – the sentence given will always be in your favor!

SONYA MILLS-McCALL, MSgt (Ret.)
United States Air Force
(1982 – 2008)

Sonya Mills-McCall is a disabled veteran having served 26 years in the United States Air Force reaching the rank of Master Sergeant (E-7). Sonya's military training skills, dedication, and professionalism propel her as a strategist, innovator, visionary, and planner. She is well-known for being proactive, flexible, diverse, organizational, relational, managing projects, and transforming a plain room into an elaborate one.

Prior to Sonya's current position of Administrative Assistant to the Pastor, she worked in several capacities such as Command Post Controller for 187th Fighter Wing, Air National Guard, and Chaplain Assistant for National Guard Bureau Chief of Chaplains.

Sonya is the owner of AWSM Event Planning & Catering, an independent Mary Kay Consultant, a member of Women of Will (W.O.W.) Women Impacting & Lifting Lives, Fortitude Leadership Academy, and she serves on the Board of LEAD Academy Charter School Montgomery, Alabama.

Sonya enjoys making a difference in the lives of others, cooking, working tirelessly, traveling, spending quality time with family and friends, and most of all spoiling her grandchildren. She currently utilizes her business, leadership, time management, and organizational skills to ensure "AWeSoMe Professional Service is Provided" to those she serves. Having been a teenage mom she strives to inspire and enable young ladies to be all they can be.

Sonya, an Alabama native, has four beautiful children: Tara (Raymond) Marlow, Tavien Feaster, the late Colin Conner, and Tene' Walton, and 12 precious grandchildren; Raymond, Torin, Briana, Dasia, DaKiya, Christian, Carson, Junior, Johnai, Carlos, Calece, and Joelle. GOD IS GOOD!

YOU ARE STRONGER THAN YOU COULD EVER IMAGINE

Erin Owens Weatherly

My military journey started in college. I attended North Carolina Agricultural and Technical State University, majoring in Architectural Engineering. Growing up, my father said he wasn't paying for my college, nor wedding because I would put more effort into it. So, I hustled getting scholarships, grants, and loans. Unfortunately, it still wasn't enough as an out-of-state University Student. I ended up working three jobs to help pay for room and board, tuition, meals, school supplies, etc. One day, I found out the ROTC department had a new program...you could join in your junior or senior year with the Air Force or Army Detachment and the military would pay a student's tuition. All I heard was money, money, money. I inherited an adventurous spirit from my mom and was willing to try anything once. My friends thought I was absolutely CRAZY to join ROTC as a rising senior and told me to watch *Saving Private Ryan* first, then make my decision about joining ROTC (well, I still have watched that movie to this day). The Commandant Commander stated I could try the program out for a semester and commit to it later. The ROTC course was challenging, but very intriguing. The following semester, I signed on the dotted-line and that decision changed my life forever.

Eight days after my commissioning ceremony and graduation, I started work as a Second Lieutenant in the 11th Civil Engineer Squadron at Bolling AFB, Washington, DC. Since I was only in the ROTC program for a short time, there were still a lot of things I did not know as new officer of the United States Air Force. At this young stage in my career, I learned behind every good officer is an EXCELLENT non-commissioned officer. Two men that ensured a "snotty-nose-fresh-out-of-school" Lieutenant stayed on the right track were two Non-Commissioned Officers (NCO). These two men provided insight on everyday situations that was oblivious to me. In addition, there was another person that was very influential to me in the 11th Civil Engineer Squadron, and it was my squadron commander. She was the first female African American commander I saw and was ecstatic she was my boss! That was the first time that I saw myself in a major leadership role in the military and could one day be in her shoes. Having this commander as my supervisor fostered my first professional goal of becoming a squadron commander. Actually, it was not only my goal, but a DREAM of mine. As I continued my career, I was mentored on achievable milestones that could showcase my accomplishments in my records through assignments, awards, decorations etc. The mentorship helped me on the road towards becoming a commander. I also learned that every mentor does NOT have to look like you, and it was great to learn valuable lessons from all of them.

God knows the desire of your heart, and He blessed me with a command position in June 2017 and a joint assignment with my husband so our family of three would not be separated. I felt like I finally made it. After so many years of deployments, TDYs, late nights, "overtime" work, etc., I finally got what I deserve and earned...being a commander of a squadron. I knew I was in a key role to help make the Air Force a better organization and make a difference to Airmen (military and civilian) lives. My sense of purpose was refined, and I felt like I had arrived. It was not an easy job, but I know, other than being a mom, it was going to be the best hardest job in my career.

Being a squadron commander was a major adjustment for my family. My husband had to pick up additional duties around the house to assist with our 1-year-old daughter and I had to live with the mom-guilt and wife-guilt for not being "present" many days for my spouse and daughter. I learned command takes up a lot of your time as you are guiding your new "family" (your squadron). I was blessed to inherit a squadron that was motivated to improve the processes on the base, and I trusted their leadership. Likewise, throughout my career, I have trusted my leadership team because they were able to provide honest feedback and opinions on my efforts and accomplishments. As the squadron commander, our organization won numerous quarterly and annual awards across the base, earned the City of Cheyenne award, had a robust Military

Spouse program, and was active in the community through community service and professional development. I was very proud of my squadron and their accomplishments.

In April 2018, I was notified through my Unit Deployment Manager (UDM) that I was selected for a deployment as a Deputy Group Commander. As much as I didn't want to leave my husband and daughter, it would be a great experience to understand the responsibilities as a Group Commander. Becoming a Group Commander was an additional professional goal for my career. Unfortunately, the Wing Commander provided a response called a *reclama* to state I could not fill the deployment position because my position on base as a squadron commander was too valuable to leave the installation and provided four different reasons. I was disappointed I would not be able to use my skills for the new position down range but relieved I didn't have to leave my family.

On 2 May 2018, after the National Prayer Breakfast event, my supervisor requested I come to her office for a meeting. I contacted my supervisor's front office staff to ask how I should prepare for the meeting and the Executive and Deputy instructed me to just show up. When I reported to her office and sat in the chair across from her desk, she stared reading a memorandum out loud to me stating she was relieving from command...in other words, she was firing me. My mind was racing as she continued to read. I was thinking to myself this was a bad dream and I have to wake up. Then I was thinking she had to be kidding because she never once stated she was not pleased with my work or efforts through conversation, emails, nor formal feedbacks. Lastly, I was thinking what did I do to deserve this treatment. As she finished reading the memorandum, her last statement was "I could not contact anyone from my squadron for 90 days and a Chaplain was standing outside the building if I needed to talk to someone." Just like that, my world changed. And my mind immediately told myself that I wasn't good enough and I was a failure. Since I was still in shock, how can I have a stellar career for the last 17 years, and someone can easily throw away my career with a whip of the pen and never explained how my actions equated to being relieved of command.

Over the next three months, I remained on the base before moving to another base. I felt humiliated, embarrassed, and exhausted. I would constantly run into people, and they would ask, "What happened?" The only way I could respond was, "I don't know!" It was also seeing personnel from my squadron and not being able to shake their hand to say "Hello" or give a hug to say, "Thanks for being an awesome Airman in my squadron." I had the largest squadron on base, and I would have to fight this battle daily. But I couldn't let the Wing leadership steal my joy. Even after several articles were written about my dismissal in various news outlet, like the Air Force Times, I continued to keep my head high and smile, even though I was crying in my husband's arms every night.

However, a powerful quote I remembered during this situation that kept playing in my mind was, "A man's rejection is God's protection." God was definitely protecting me and my family from the toxic leadership I was experiencing. He knew the desire of my heart by letting me enjoy my goal for over 16 years to finally become a squadron commander. However, staying in that location would have destroyed me, my marriage, and my family. It appeared God was giving me a "timeout." Timeout is defined as a time for rest or recreation away from one's usual work or studies, a halt on the play. This was an opportunity to repurpose the "play" and He used it to sit me down to restore me to ensure I do not lose my focus. This unfortunate situation stopped me dead in my tracks and I did not allow it to help me grow until years later.

Every "coach" calls new plays when necessary, and they never ask the players if they like the new play, because the coach just doesn't care what the player thinks, and the coach knows what is best for the team/player. I was so worried about being relieved of command, wondered what people thought of me. I was angry with the Air Force and was trying to figure out how could I retain a positive image. I was not able to let go of the hurt and I "waddled" in my pain for years. My sorrow and pain were controlling my life and I was constantly stuck in a bad place. My misery was controlling me, and it was hard getting out of it. There are coaches that would say that a player can't play well when they are mad because they can't make the right decision. I wasn't always thinking positively and thankfully I finally sought professional help to get through that rough season in my life.

The biggest question I had to ask myself was, "Now that I have had the time to reflect, what did I gain during the removal of command and my "timeout" from God? What do I do after the moment?" Joseph stated in Genesis 50:20 to his brothers, *"You meant evil against me, but God used it or good."* Romans 8:28 also states, *"And we know that for those who love God, all things work together for good, for those who are called according to his purpose."* My experience as a commander didn't totally crush me, but it did have me drop to my knees plenty of times to ask why. But then my statement to myself was, "Why not me?" God trusted me enough to go through this situation and trust Him to deliver me from it. I was hardheaded and wasn't listening to Him sooner, but I was blessed with family and friends to also help me through. God always provides a support system to get you through tough situations. During those years, I rested, I cried, and I got up, and I finally moved on. I am now learning I have to be fearless so I can get through it and not get off track. I actually thank God for that moment in my life. It gave me substance and I didn't realize the strength He had given me.

As I conclude, there is a light at the end of the tunnel. My husband and I are still married and our family is intact. We are now expecting our son in a couple of months, and we are so excited to build His Kingdom with more saints. We were able to move back to San Antonio and be planted back with our church. I left that toxic leadership to supervisors that did not judge me on my past but judged me on the work they encountered. I am still in counseling to improve myself for me and my family.

Lastly, on 10 September 2021, I finally filed an IG Complaint towards the Wing Leadership. Even though I do not know how this will end, I am glad I am finally using my voice to address a problem we have in the Air Force and the power leadership has to ruin a career without justification. I have asked for a review by a panel of the Air Force Policies, the right to wear my commander's badge, and an opportunity to command again. My support system stated they were proud of me, but I am proud of myself for using God's strength in me to voice this problem. I know I am speaking for people who didn't have the time or resources for their own fight. Through it all, I didn't know I was this strong…but He has given me the courage to not give up.

ERIN OWENS WEATHERLY, Lt. Col.
United States Air Force
*Operation Enduring Freedom, Operation Iraqi Freedom,
Operation New Dawn, Operation Welcome Allies*
2001 – Present

Erin Owens Weatherly is an Active-Duty Air Force Civil Engineer Officer that works for Air Force Installation and Mission Support Center. As a Lieutenant Colonel, she has served most recently as the Chief of Strategic Basing and Beddown. Lt. Col. Weatherly was commissioned in 2001 through ROTC program at North Carolina Agricultural & Technical State University (NC A&T SU) where she earned a degree in Architectural Engineering. Following graduation, she served in variety of engineering leadership positions in the United States and overseas military installations. Her most rewarding position during her career was a

Squadron Commander in Cheyenne, Wyoming. Some of her staff assignments include Legislative Liaison and Chief of Director Action Group.

Other than a military officer, Erin enjoys the other "hats" she wears daily. She became a member of Delta Sigma Theta Sorority, Inc. through the Alpha Mu Chapter at NC A&T SU in Spring 2001. She also became a member of the Order of Eastern Stars through the Esther P. Vaughn, Chapter #63, Osan Air Base, Republic of South Korea. She married her best friend, Lt. Col. Cedric Weatherly, in August 2012. They are proud parents of a daughter, Janelle and a son, Cedric, Jr. In addition to keeping busy as a mother and a wife, Erin enjoys being active in volunteer work in the community, event planning, and helping out various ministries at her home church, God's Way Christian Fellowship.

About the Visionary

★ ✯ ★

Michele Irby Johnson, MSgt (Ret.)
United States Air Force
*Operation Noble Eagle, Operation Iraqi Freedom,
Operation Enduring Freedom, Operation New Dawn*
(1986 – 2012)

Michele Irby Johnson is a retired, disabled Veteran who is an Energetic Motivational and Transformational Speaker and Trainer as well as a Certified Life Coach who is a much sought-after voice who serves the Abused, Women, Non-Profits, Family and Education, Veterans, and Faith-Based communities through her unique style that reaches deep into the hearts and lives of those longing for transformation, elevation, inspiration, and empowerment. Michele has a great love for seeing people's lives changed. Through speaking, training, coaching, and mentoring, she gets joy in developing and elevating people to a place of greatness, seeing them reach their goals, and helping them to see their tomorrow through the lens of who they were called to be in this world.

As a speaker and trainer, Michele commands the stage to captivate her audience through animated storytelling, humor, wisdom, and authenticity. She understands that she is on the platform to impart and to transfer what the audience needs beyond the conclusion of the event. She injects herself into the moment and shifts the atmosphere prompting listeners to decide what is important to them, how they should respond, and if they want to enact change in their lives or in the businesses.

Michele is the visionary for the **Arise and Inspire Speaker's Bootcamp** which provides a four-day, eight-hour intensive training experience where amateur speakers can learn the tools and techniques needed to mount the stage as a speaker. Once attendees have completed the bootcamp, they are invited to participate in the two-day **Arise and Inspire Speaker's Summit**, where they share their stories before an in-person and virtual audience, with opportunities to acquire speaking engagements, new clients, and a connection to a network of experienced speakers.

Michele's gift as a transformation architect has afforded her the opportunity to serve surrounding regions through speaking, preaching, retreats, conferences, and teaching workshops and seminars on Domestic Violence to such groups as educators, medical personnel, clergy, women's ministries, and youth alike. Her capacity has allowed her travel and serve in such areas as Maryland, Washington, DC, Virginia, North Carolina, Alabama, Tennessee, Florida, Texas, Guam, Southwest Asia, and Africa.

As a survivor of Domestic Violence and an advocate against Domestic Violence, Michele penned her first literary work entitled *"Love's TKO: A Testimony of Abuse, Victory and Healing,"* which shares her experiences as a victim of a love gone bad through domestic violence. To continue her love for writing and reaching others through this gift, she also penned *"Grace For Your Journey: Sermons of Survival in the Wilderness."* She is a best-selling Co-Author of the anthology "*Women Inspiring Nations Volume 3: I'm Still Standing.*" She was the visionary on the anthology project *"In Recovery: Rising From the Ruins"* and she has several other literary works in progress that she believes will prove beneficial to the reader from personal, emotional, and spiritual perspectives.

As an educator, Michele has served as an Adjunct Professor at a state university, teaching Life & Health classes to undergraduate students; and teaching Counseling Women and Domestic Violence Crisis Counseling (two courses she wrote) to graduate students. She is the Founder, Director, and Instructor for Kingdom Covenant Bible Institute, where the mission focuses on teaching and training disciples according to Matthew 28:19-20. She is also passionate about helping people be administratively prepared for the inevitability of death. As a bereavement liaison and consultant, she has written and delivers Estate Planning webinars and workshops to specialized groups, organizations, churches, families, and individuals. She firmly believes that having such affairs in order is a great display of a legacy of love one can leave behind for their families. Her vision is to provide peace of mind for your future.

Michele holds five degrees: Master of Arts in Counseling (Crisis Response and Trauma); Master of Arts in Human Resource Development; a Bachelor of Science in the field of Human Resource Management; as well as two Associates Degrees from the Community College of the Air Force: One in Education and Training and the other in Social Services. She retired from the USAF after 26 years of combined dedicated military service with the 113th DC Air National Guard at Andrews Air Force Base. Michele is affiliated with Veterans-N-Transition, Transformation Academy, Apostolic Grace Evangelistic Fellowship, Speaker Hub, Fair Consulting, Association of Christians in Leadership (Advisor), to name a few. She also hosts her own Virtual Talk Show: *"Life Matters with Michele,"* which airs weekly on Facebook LIVE and is also posted on her YouTube Channel Life Matters with Michele TV Official.

In April 2020, Michele started the Grace Point Radio Broadcast with her husband, Apostle Shaun P. Johnson, Sr. on the DMV Power Gospel Radio Network. She now broadcasts **Grace Point** on its own YouTube Channel Grace Point TV Official and on Sensational Sounds Radio weekly, both platforms taking to heart the necessity to spread the Gospel to all the world in hopes of introducing the lost to Jesus Christ, reclaiming the backslider, and to minister comfort, strength, encouragement, and healing to the brokenhearted.

As an entrepreneur, Michele's countless skills translate beyond her speaking, training, and coaching arenas as she helps entrepreneurs, educators, authors, clergy, institutions of higher learning, and community leaders to realize their vision by providing virtual assistant services that ease the burden of the cumbersome, day-to-day tasks that often hinder forward movement and success. Her goal is to get individuals and organizations back to productivity and profitability by adding value to their lives through time and project management, administrative support, and curriculum and training development.

As a springboard to their love for literary work, Michele and her husband have launched a self-publishing consulting business that helps authors to fulfill their dream of being published. They offer design services, project management, editorial services, and more.

In her spare time, Michele enjoys watching HGTV, A Different World, Living Single, the Golden Girls, and any type of Cold Case, Forensic Files, or crime shows and spending time with her husband, Shaun P. Johnson, Sr. Together, they have three sons, one daughter, and one grandson.

Connect with Michele
Facebook/LinkedIn: Michele Irby Johnson
Instagram: Michele.irby.75
www.iam-mij.com
www.optimumpvs.com
www.onekingdompublishing.com
www.livingbygraceministries.org
www.kingdomcbi.org
YouTube: Grace Point TV Official
YouTube: Life Matters with Michele TV Official

Other Literary Works by the Visionary

Love's TKO:
A Testimony of Abuse, Victory and Healing

Grace for Your Journey:
Sermons of Survival in the Wilderness

<u>Visionary Anthology Projects</u>

In Recovery: Rising From the Ruins
Stories of Restoration and Resilience

Boots and Beyond:
Stories of Trials, Tragedy, Triumph and Transition

My Bald Is Beautiful:
I Am not My Hair
(Releasing December 2021)

Contributing Author in the following literary work:

Women Inspiring Nations Volume 3:
I'm Still Standing